PENGUIN STUDENT EDITIONS

# TEN SHORT STORIES

Roald Dahl's parents were Norwegian, but he was born in Wales in 1916 and went to school in England. On the outbreak of the Second World War, he enlisted in the Royal Air Force at Nairobi. He was severely wounded after joining a fighter squadron in Libya, but later served as a fighter pilot in Greece and Syria. His first short stories, based on his wartime experiences, were originally published in American magazines and afterwards as a book, *Over to You*. Since then his stories have been widely translated and have become bestsellers all over the world. Dahl also published two volumes of autobiography, *Boy* and *Going Solo*, a much-praised novel, *My Uncle Oswald*, and *Roald Dahl's Book of Ghost Stories*, of which he was editor. During the last year of his life he compiled a book of anecdotes and recipes with his wife, which was published as *Roald Dahl's Cookbook*. One of the most successful and well known of all children's writers, his books are read by children all over the world. These include *James and the Giant Peach*, *Charlie and the Chocolate Factory*, *The Twits*, *The Witches*, *The BFG* and *Matilda*. Roald Dahl died in November 1990. *The Times* described him as 'one of the most widely read and influential writers of our generation'.

Ronald Carter is Professor of Modern English Language in the School of English Studies, University of Nottingham. He has published widely in the field of language and literature studies and applied linguistics and English teaching. He is the co-author with John McRae of *The Penguin Guide to English Literature* (1996) and *The Routledge History of Literature in English: Britain and Ireland* (1997).

John McRae is Special Professor of Language in Literature Studies in the School of English Studies at the University of Nottingham. He is the author or editor of more than forty books and has lectured in over forty countries worldwide.

Penguin Student Editions

Series editors: Ronald Carter and John McRae

**Other titles in this series:**

# Roald Dahl

# **Ten Short Stories**

Edited by Ronald Carter

PENGUIN BOOKS

PENGUIN BOOKS

Published by the Penguin Group
Penguin Books Ltd, 27 Wrights Lane, London w8 5tz, England
Penguin Putnam Inc., 375 Hudson Street, New York, New York 10014, USA
Penguin Books Australia Ltd, Ringwood, Victoria, Australia
Penguin Books Canada Ltd, 10 Alcorn Avenue, Toronto, Ontario, Canada m4v 3b2
Penguin Books (NZ) Ltd, Private Bag 102902, NSMC, Auckland, New Zealand

Penguin Books Ltd, Registered Offices: Harmondsworth, Middlesex, England

Published in Penguin Student Editions 2000
10 9 8 7 6 5 4 3 2 1

'The Umbrella Man', 'Mr Botibol' and 'The Butler' were first published in Great
Britain by Michael Joseph Ltd in *More Tales of the Unexpected*, copyright © Roald
Dahl, 1973, 1980

The ten short stories in this book are taken from *The Collected Short Stories of Roald
Dahl*. The collection is copyright © Felicity Dahl and the other Executors of the
Estate of Roald Dahl, 1991

Introduction and Notes copyright © Ronald Carter, 2000
All rights reserved

The moral right of the editor has been asserted

Set in 9.75/12.5 pt PostScript Monotype Plantin
Typeset by Rowland Phototypesetting Ltd, Bury St Edmunds, Suffolk
Printed in England by Clays Ltd, St Ives plc

# Contents

# Introduction

Roald Dahl was born in 1916 in Llandaff, a small town just outside Cardiff, the capital city of Wales. Dahl's parents were Norwegian, the family having originally moved from Norway to Wales in the 1880s. His name is Norwegian and his first name Roald is pronounced 'Roo-ahl' with a silent final 'd'. Roald's father, Harald, worked in the shipping industry and the family were prosperous, living in a large house in the Glamorgan countryside. Dahl's mother, Sophie, was Harald's second wife and Roald was her only son. Dahl was only four years old at the time of his father's death and when his father died, Dahl felt as if he became an only child, even though he had sisters and step-brothers and step-sisters. Many of his stories have children as the heroes or heroines or as the main point of view for the story and they are nearly always alone, without brothers and sisters to whom they can talk and in whom they can confide.

Roald Dahl led a rather lonely life as a child. He writes in some detail about growing up and about his childhood in South Wales in his autobiography *Boy* which was published in 1984. His schooldays until his eighteenth year were spent at a boys' public school, Repton, in Derbyshire. According to many accounts Dahl's schooldays were not always happy and he was subjected to much teasing and bullying by other boys on account of his strange name, and his height. Roald Dahl was six foot six inches tall. Many of his stories, especially stories for children, explore the theme of bullies and bullying.

After leaving school Dahl travelled extensively and in 1934 joined the multi-national oil company Shell. He worked both in London and in East Africa. On the outbreak of war he joined the Royal Air Force and was based in Nairobi, Kenya, eventually joining a fighter squadron in Libya in North Africa. It was while flying with this squadron, during which time he fought as a pilot in Syria and Greece, that he was severely wounded. In 1942 he went to Washington where he worked in the Embassy. He was subsequently transferred to Intelligence work. It was in Washington that he began to write his first short stories.

Roald Dahl's short stories have been bestsellers all over the world and have been translated into many languages. The books in which they are collected are *Someone Like You*, *Kiss Kiss*, *Switch Bitch*, *Twenty-nine Kisses from Roald Dahl*, *Over To You* and *Ah! Sweet Mystery of Life*. Several stories have also been collected under more general headings such as *Tales of the Unexpected* and *More Tales of the Unexpected*. Several stories of the 'unexpected' were dramatized for television and have made his writings even more popular throughout the world.

The use of the word 'unexpected' in relation to many of Roald Dahl's short stories is quite common. The endings to his stories are often unexpected and take the reader by surprise. Sometimes the endings are comic, sometimes they are tragic, sometimes a likeable character wins, sometimes an evil and disliked character wins; in most cases, however, the ending is almost impossible to predict and there is a 'twist-in-the-tail'. Many of the stories are humorous as characters find themselves in unusual or extreme situations but the humour is nearly always a 'black' humour because comic and tragic elements mix together.

Black humour is an important element in Roald Dahl's writings. Dahl seems to enjoy treating some of his characters in a cruel way. The characters find themselves in circumstances which they did not expect or which have tragic consequences, but their situation is often described in an amusing way and readers find that they are laughing at the personal tragedies of the character and that they may even enjoy reading about their misfortunes. Black humour is directed at characters who are shown to be unsympathetic but is also sometimes reserved for characters we have grown to like. The starting-point for many of the stories is often everyday, common incidents of ordinary life and the characters are often people with whom readers can identify. Not one of Roald Dahl's stories could be called sentimental.

Roald Dahl first met his first wife in London in 1951. Patricia Neal was an American and was by then already established as a successful stage and film actress and Dahl was not yet recognized as a writer, though at that time he was writing almost full-time. They married in New York in July 1953. In the autumn of 1953 the collection of stories *Someone Like You* was published by the American publisher Alfred Knopf, who was to be Dahl's main publisher and supporter throughout his life, and a year later the book was published in Britain by Secker and Warburg. Roald and Patricia Dahl had four children. They divorced in 1983 and Dahl remarried Felicity Crosland.

Roald Dahl's other main publications include a highly praised novel, *My Uncle Oswald*, and a sequence of books for children which have made him one of the most famous writers of children's books in the world. His books for children include *James and the Giant Peach*, *Charlie and the Chocolate Factory*, *The Magic Finger*, *Charlie and the Great Glass Elevator*, *Fantastic Mr Fox*, *The Twits*, *The Witches*, *The BFG* (the initials stand for 'big friendly giant') and *Matilda*. *The Witches* was the 1983 winner of the Whitbread Award. Many people believe that these children's stories will be the classics of the future. In Britain alone, between 1980 and 1990, over eleven million of his books were sold in paperback form. The figure is considerably more than the total number of children born in Britain in these years. These books for children helped considerably to make Roald Dahl a multi-millionaire.

Several of Dahl's books have been made into films. *Danny* (from *Danny, Champion of the World*) and *The Witches* were made into films in the 1980s. Roald Dahl himself was interested in the writing of film scripts and was involved in the writing of the internationally successful film *Chitty Chitty Bang Bang*. He also worked to adapt *Charlie and the Chocolate Factory* for the screen and in 1971 it was released as the film *Willy Wonka and the Chocolate Factory*.

Roald Dahl died in November 1990. He is buried in Great Missenden in Berkshire which had been his main family home for most of his adult life. He is one of the most widely read and influential writers of the past fifty years.

# Chronology

## Roald Dahl's Life

**1916**  Roald Dahl is born in Llandaff, S. Wales.

**1934**  Leaves Repton School, Derbyshire, and joins international oil company, Shell.

**1953**  Marries first wife, actress Patricia Neal.
**1953**  Dahl's first collection of stories, *Someone Like You*, is published.

**1964**  Dahl's best-known children's story, *Charlie and the Chocolate Factory*, is published.

**1971**  The film *Willy Wonka and the Chocolate Factory*, based on the novel of 1964, is released.
**1979–80**  Two collections of his stories *Tales of the Unexpected* and *More Tales of the Unexpected* are published.
**1980–90**  Some of Dahl's most successful children's stories are published, including *The BFG* (1982), *The Witches* (1983), *Matilda* (1988).

**Roald Dahl's Times**

**1914–18**   First World War.

**1922**   James Joyce, *Ulysses* and T. S. Eliot, *The Waste Land*.
**1933**   Adolf Hitler comes to power in Germany.

**1939–45**   Second World War.

**1954**   William Golding, *Lord of the Flies*.
**1963**   The assassination of President Kennedy shocks the Western World.
**1964–70**   London becomes the worldwide capital of youth culture – especially music, clothes and design.
**1969**   US astronauts land on the moon.
**1971**   Britain joins the EEC (European Economic Community).

**1979**   Margaret Thatcher begins an eleven-year term as British Prime Minister.

**1983**  Dahl remarries. His second wife is Felicity Crosland.

**1984**  His autobiography, *Boy*, is published.

**1990**  Roald Dahl dies and is buried in Great Missenden, Berkshire.

**1989**  Cold War between America/the West and the Soviet Union/ Eastern Europe comes to an end. Capitalism begins to extend eastwards.

# Ten Short Stories

# The Umbrella Man

I'm going to tell you about a funny thing that happened to my 🎧
mother and me yesterday evening. I am twelve years old and I'm
a girl. My mother is thirty-four but I am nearly as tall as her already.

Yesterday afternoon, my mother took me up to London to see
the dentist. He found one hole. It was in a back tooth and he filled 5
it without hurting me too much. After that, we went to a café. I
had a banana split and my mother had a cup of coffee. By the time
we got up to leave, it was about six o'clock.

When we came out of the café it had started to rain. 'We must
get a taxi,' my mother said. We were wearing ordinary hats and 10
coats, and it was raining quite hard.

'Why don't we go back into the café and wait for it to stop?' I
said. I wanted another of those banana splits. They were gorgeous.

'It isn't going to stop,' my mother said. 'We must get home.'

We stood on the pavement in the rain, looking for a taxi. Lots 15
of them came by but they all had passengers inside them. 'I wish
we had a car with a chauffeur,' my mother said.

Just then a man came up to us. He was a small man and he was
pretty old, probably seventy or more. He raised his hat politely and
said to my mother, 'Excuse me, I do hope you will excuse me . . .' 20
He had a fine white moustache and bushy white eyebrows and a
wrinkly pink face. He was sheltering under an umbrella which he
held high over his head.

'Yes?' my mother said, very cool and distant.

'I wonder if I could ask a small favour of you,' he said. 'It is only 25
a very small favour.'

I saw my mother looking at him suspiciously. She is a suspicious

person, my mother. She is especially suspicious of two things –
strange men and boiled eggs. When she cuts the top off a boiled
egg, she pokes around inside it with her spoon as though expecting
to find a mouse or something. With strange men, she has a golden
5  rule which says, 'The nicer the man seems to be, the more suspicious
you must become.' This little old man was particularly nice. He
was polite. He was well-spoken. He was well-dressed. He was a
real gentleman. The reason I knew he was a gentleman was because
of his shoes. 'You can always spot a gentleman by the shoes he
10 wears,' was another of my mother's favourite sayings. This man
had beautiful brown shoes.

'The truth of the matter is,' the little man was saying, 'I've got
myself into a bit of a scrape. I need some help. Not much I assure
you. It's almost nothing, in fact, but I do need it. You see, madam,
15 old people like me often become terribly forgetful . . .'

My mother's chin was up and she was staring down at him along
the full length of her nose. It was a fearsome thing, this frosty-nosed
stare of my mother's. Most people go to pieces completely when
she gives it to them. I once saw my own headmistress begin to
20 stammer and simper like an idiot when my mother gave her a really
foul frosty-noser. But the little man on the pavement with the
umbrella over his head didn't bat an eyelid. He gave a gentle smile
and said, 'I beg you to believe, madam, that I am not in the habit
of stopping ladies in the street and telling them my troubles.'

25 'I should hope not,' my mother said.

I felt quite embarrassed by my mother's sharpness. I wanted to
say to her, 'Oh, mummy, for heaven's sake, he's a very very old
man, and he's sweet and polite, and he's in some sort of trouble,
so don't be so beastly to him.' But I didn't say anything.

30 The little man shifted his umbrella from one hand to the other.
'I've never forgotten it before,' he said.

'You've never forgotten what?' my mother asked sternly.

'My wallet,' he said. 'I must have left it in my other jacket. Isn't
that the silliest thing to do?'

35 'Are you asking me to give you money?' my mother said.

'Oh, good gracious me, no!' he cried. 'Heaven forbid I should ever do that!'

'Then what *are* you asking?' my mother said. 'Do hurry up. We're getting soaked to the skin here.'

'I know you are,' he said. 'And that is why I'm offering you this umbrella of mine to protect you, and to keep forever, if . . . if only . . .'

'If only what?' my mother said.

'If only you would give me in return a pound for my taxi-fare just to get me home.'

My mother was still suspicious. 'If you had no money in the first place,' she said, 'then how did you get here?'

'I walked,' he answered. 'Every day I go for a lovely long walk and then I summon a taxi to take me home. I do it every day of the year.'

'Why don't you walk home now?' my mother asked.

'Oh, I wish I could,' he said. 'I do wish I could. But I don't think I could manage it on these silly old legs of mine. I've gone too far already.'

My mother stood there chewing her lower lip. She was beginning to melt a bit, I could see that. And the idea of getting an umbrella to shelter under must have tempted her a good deal.

'It's a lovely umbrella,' the little man said.

'So I've noticed,' my mother said.

'It's silk,' he said.

'I can see that.'

'Then why don't you take it, madam,' he said. 'It cost me over twenty pounds, I promise you. But that's of no importance so long as I can get home and rest these old legs of mine.'

I saw my mother's hand feeling for the clasp of her purse. She saw me watching her. I was giving her one of my *own* frosty-nosed looks this time and she knew exactly what I was telling her. Now listen, mummy, I was telling her, you simply *mustn't* take advantage of a tired old man in this way. It's a rotten thing to do. My mother paused and looked back at me. Then she said to the little man, 'I don't think it's quite right that I should take an umbrella from you worth twenty pounds. I think I'd better just *give* you the taxi-fare and be done with it.'

'No, no no!' he cried. 'It's out of the question! I wouldn't dream
5 of it! Not in a million years! I would never accept money from you like that! Take the umbrella, dear lady, and keep the rain off your shoulders!'

My mother gave me a triumphant sideways look. There you are, she was telling me. You're wrong. He *wants* me to have it.

10 She fished into her purse and took out a pound note. She held it out to the little man. He took it and handed her the umbrella. He pocketed the pound, raised his hat, gave a quick bow from the waist, and said, 'Thank you, madam, thank you.' Then he was gone.

15 'Come under here and keep dry, darling,' my mother said. 'Aren't we lucky. I've never had a silk umbrella before. I couldn't afford it.'

'Why were you so horrid to him in the beginning?' I asked.

'I wanted to satisfy myself he wasn't a trickster,' she said. 'And
20 I did. He was a gentleman. I'm very pleased I was able to help him.'

'Yes, mummy,' I said.

'A *real* gentleman,' she went on. 'Wealthy, too, otherwise he wouldn't have had a silk umbrella. I shouldn't be surprised if he
25 isn't a titled person. Sir Harry Goldsworthy or something like that.'

'Yes, mummy.'

'This will be a good lesson to you,' she went on. 'Never rush things. Always take your time when you are summing someone up. Then you'll never make mistakes.'

30 'There he goes,' I said. 'Look.'

'Where?'

'Over there. He's crossing the street. Goodness, mummy, what a hurry he's in.'

We watched the little man as he dodged nimbly in and out of
35 the traffic. When he reached the other side of the street, he turned left, walking very fast.

'He doesn't look very tired to me, does he to you, mummy?'

My mother didn't answer.

'He doesn't look as though he's trying to get a taxi, either,' I said.

My mother was standing very still and stiff, staring across the street at the little man. We could see him clearly. He was in a terrific hurry. He was bustling along the pavement, sidestepping the other pedestrians and swinging his arms like a soldier on the march.

'He's up to something,' my mother said, stony-faced.

'But what?'

'I don't know,' my mother snapped. 'But I'm going to find out. Come with me.' She took my arm and we crossed the street together. Then we turned left.

'Can you see him?' my mother asked.

'Yes. There he is. He's turning right down the next street.'

We came to the corner and turned right. The little man was about twenty yards ahead of us. He was scuttling along like a rabbit and we had to walk very fast to keep up with him. The rain was pelting down harder than ever now and I could see it dripping from the brim of his hat on to his shoulders. But we were snug and dry under our lovely big silk umbrella.

'What *is* he up to?' my mother said.

'What if he turns round and sees us?' I asked.

'I don't care if he does,' my mother said. 'He lied to us. He said he was too tired to walk any further and he's practically running us off our feet! He's a barefaced liar! He's a crook!'

'You mean he's *not* a titled gentleman?' I asked.

'Be quiet,' she said.

At the next crossing, the little man turned right again.

Then he turned left.

Then right.

'I'm not giving up now,' my mother said.

'He's disappeared!' I cried. 'Where's he gone?'

'He went in that door!' my mother said. 'I saw him! Into that house! Great heavens, it's a pub!'

It was a pub. In big letters right across the front it said THE RED
LION.

'You're not going in are you, mummy?'

'No,' she said. 'We'll watch from outside.'

5    There was a big plate-glass window along the front of the pub,
and although it was a bit steamy on the inside, we could see through
it very well if we went close.

We stood huddled together outside the pub window. I was
clutching my mother's arm. The big raindrops were making a loud
10 noise on our umbrella. 'There he is,' I said. 'Over there.'

The room we were looking into was full of people and cigarette
smoke, and our little man was in the middle of it all. He was now
without his hat and coat, and he was edging his way through the
crowd towards the bar. When he reached it, he placed both hands
15 on the bar itself and spoke to the barman. I saw his lips moving as
he gave his order. The barman turned away from him for a few
seconds and came back with a smallish tumbler filled to the brim
with light brown liquid. The little man placed a pound note on the
counter.

20    'That's my pound!' my mother hissed. 'By golly, he's got a
nerve!'

'What's in the glass?' I asked.

'Whisky,' my mother said. 'Neat whisky.'

The barman didn't give him any change from the pound.

25    'That must be a treble whisky,' my mummy said.

'What's a treble?' I asked.

'Three times the normal measure,' she answered.

The little man picked up the glass and put it to his lips. He tilted
it gently. Then he tilted it higher . . . and higher . . . and higher . . .
30 and very soon all the whisky had disappeared down his throat in
one long pour.

'That's a jolly expensive drink,' I said.

'It's ridiculous!' my mummy said. 'Fancy paying a pound for
something to swallow in one go!'

35    'It cost him more than a pound,' I said. 'It cost him a twenty-
pound silk umbrella.'

'So it did,' my mother said. 'He must be mad.'

The little man was standing by the bar with the empty glass in his hand. He was smiling now, and a sort of golden glow of pleasure was spreading over his round pink face. I saw his tongue come out to lick the white moustache, as though searching for one last drop of that precious whisky.

Slowly, he turned away from the bar and edged his way back through the crowd to where his hat and coat were hanging. He put on his hat. He put on his coat. Then, in a manner so superbly cool and casual that you hardly noticed anything at all, he lifted from the coat-rack one of the many wet umbrellas hanging there, and off he went.

'Did you see that!' my mother shrieked. 'Did you see what he did!'

'Ssshh!' I whispered. 'He's coming out!'

We lowered our umbrella to hide our faces, and peered out from under it.

Out he came. But he never looked in our direction. He opened his new umbrella over his head and scurried off down the road the way he had come.

'So that's his little game!' my mother said.

'Neat,' I said. 'Super.'

We followed him back to the main street where we had first met him, and we watched him as he proceeded, with no trouble at all, to exchange his new umbrella for another pound note. This time it was with a tall thin fellow who didn't even have a coat or hat. And as soon as the transaction was completed, our little man trotted off down the street and was lost in the crowd. But this time he went in the opposite direction.

'You see how clever he is!' my mother said. 'He never goes to the same pub twice!'

'He could go on doing this all night,' I said.

'Yes,' my mother said. 'Of course. But I'll bet he prays like mad for rainy days.'

# Dip in the Pool

On the morning of the third day, the sea calmed. Even the most delicate passengers – those who had not been seen around the ship since sailing time – emerged from their cabins and crept on to the sun deck where the deck steward gave them chairs and tucked rugs around their legs and left them lying in rows, their faces upturned to the pale, almost heatless January sun.

It had been moderately rough the first two days, and this sudden calm and the sense of comfort that it brought created a more genial atmosphere over the whole ship. By the time evening came, the passengers, with twelve hours of good weather behind them, were beginning to feel confident, and at eight o'clock that night the main dining-room was filled with people eating and drinking with the assured, complacent air of seasoned sailors.

The meal was not half over when the passengers became aware, by the slight friction between their bodies and the seats of their chairs, that the big ship had actually started rolling again. It was very gentle at first, just a slow, lazy leaning to one side, then to the other, but it was enough to cause a subtle, immediate change of mood over the whole room. A few of the passengers glanced up from their food, hesitating, waiting, almost listening for the next roll, smiling nervously, little secret glimmers of apprehension in their eyes. Some were completely unruffled, some were openly smug, a number of the smug ones making jokes about food and weather in order to torture the few who were beginning to suffer. The movement of the ship then became rapidly more and more violent, and only five or six minutes after the first roll had been noticed, she was swinging heavily from side to side, the passengers bracing themselves in their chairs, leaning against the pull as in a car cornering.

At last the really bad roll came, and Mr William Botibol, sitting at the purser's table, saw his plate of poached turbot with hollandaise sauce sliding suddenly away from under his fork. There was a flutter of excitement, everybody reaching for plates and wineglasses. Mrs Renshaw, seated at the purser's right, gave a little scream and clutched that gentleman's arm.

'Going to be a dirty night,' the purser said, looking at Mrs Renshaw. 'I think it's blowing up for a very dirty night.'

There was just the faintest suggestion of relish in the way the purser said this.

A steward came hurrying up and sprinkled water on the table cloth between the plates. The excitement subsided. Most of the passengers continued with their meal. A small number, including Mrs Renshaw, got carefully to their feet and threaded their ways with a kind of concealed haste between the tables and through the doorway.

'Well,' the purser said, 'there she goes.' He glanced around with approval at the remainder of his flock who were sitting quiet, looking complacent, their faces reflecting openly that extraordinary pride that travellers seem to take in being recognized as 'good sailors'.

When the eating was finished and the coffee had been served Mr Botibol, who had been unusually grave and thoughtful since the rolling started, suddenly stood up and carried his cup of coffee around to Mrs Renshaw's vacant place, next to the purser. He seated himself in the chair, then immediately leaned over and began to whisper urgently in the purser's ear. 'Excuse me,' he said, 'but could you tell me something, please?'

The purser, small and fat and red, bent forward to listen. 'What's the trouble, Mr Botibol?'

'What I want to know is this.' The man's face was anxious and the purser was watching it. 'What I want to know is will the captain already have made his estimate on the day's run – you know, for the auction pool? I mean before it began to get rough like this?'

The purser, who had prepared himself to receive a personal confidence, smiled and leaned back in his seat to relax his full belly. 'I should say so – yes,' he answered. He didn't bother to whisper his reply, although automatically he lowered his voice, as one does when answering a whisperer.

'About how long ago do you think he did it?'

'Some time this afternoon. He usually does it in the afternoon.'

'About what time?'

'Oh, I don't know. Around four o'clock I should guess.'

'Now tell me another thing. How does the captain decide which number it shall be? Does he take a lot of trouble over that?'

The purser looked at the anxious frowning face of Mr Botibol and he smiled, knowing quite well what the man was driving at. 'Well, you see, the captain has a little conference with the navigating officer, and they study the weather and a lot of other things, and then they make their estimate.'

Mr Botibol nodded, pondering this answer for a moment. Then he said, 'Do you think the captain knew there was bad weather coming today?'

'I couldn't tell you,' the purser replied. He was looking into the small black eyes of the other man, seeing the two single little specks of excitement dancing in their centres. 'I really couldn't tell you, Mr Botibol. I wouldn't know.'

'If this gets any worse it might be worth buying some of the low numbers. What do you think?' The whispering was more urgent, more anxious now.

'Perhaps it will,' the purser said. 'I doubt whether the old man allowed for a really rough night. It was pretty calm this afternoon when he made his estimate.'

The others at the table had become silent and were trying to hear, watching the purser with that intent, half-cocked, listening look that you can see also at the race track when they are trying to overhear a trainer talking about his chance: the slightly open lips, the upstretched eyebrows, the head forward and cocked a little to one side – that desperately straining, half-hypnotized, listening look that comes to all of them when they are hearing something straight from the horse's mouth.

'Now suppose *you* were allowed to buy a number, which one would *you* choose today?' Mr Botibol whispered.

'I don't know what the range is yet,' the purser patiently answered. 'They don't announce the range till the auction starts after dinner. And I'm really not very good at it anyway. I'm only the purser, you know.'

At that point Mr Botibol stood up. 'Excuse me, all,' he said, and he walked carefully away over the swaying floor between the other tables, and twice he had to catch hold of the back of a chair to steady himself against the ship's roll.

'The sun deck, please,' he said to the elevator man.

The wind caught him full in the face as he stepped out on to the open deck. He staggered and grabbed hold of the rail and held on tight with both hands, and he stood there looking out over the darkening sea where the great waves were welling up high and white horses were riding against the wind with plumes of spray behind them as they went.

'Pretty bad out there, wasn't it, sir?' the elevator man said on the way down.

Mr Botibol was combing his hair back into place with a small red comb. 'Do you think we've slackened speed at all on account of the weather?' he asked.

'Oh, my word yes, sir. We slackened off considerable since this started. You got to slacken off speed in weather like this or you'll be throwing the passengers all over the ship.'

Down in the smoking-room people were already gathering for the auction. They were grouping themselves politely around the various tables, the men a little stiff in their dinner jackets, a little pink and overshaved and stiff beside their cool white-armed women. Mr Botibol took a chair close to the auctioneer's table. He crossed his legs, folded his arms, and settled himself in his seat with the rather desperate air of a man who has made a tremendous decision and refuses to be frightened.

   The pool, he was telling himself, would probably be around seven thousand dollars. That was almost exactly what it had been the last two days with the numbers selling for between three and four hundred apiece. Being a British ship they did it in pounds,
5  but he liked to do his thinking in his own currency. Seven thousand dollars was plenty of money. My goodness, yes! And what he would do, he would get them to pay him in hundred-dollar bills and he would take it ashore in the inside pocket of his jacket. No problem there. And right away, yes right away, he would buy a Lincoln
10 convertible. He would pick it up on the way from the ship and drive it home just for the pleasure of seeing Ethel's face when she came out the front door and looked at it. Wouldn't that be something, to see Ethel's face when he glided up to the door in a brand-new pale-green Lincoln convertible! Hello, Ethel, honey,
15 he would say, speaking very casual. I just thought I'd get you a little present. I saw it in the window as I went by, so I thought of you and how you were always wanting one. You like it, honey? he would say. You like the colour? And then he would watch her face.
   The auctioneer was standing up behind his table now. 'Ladies
20 and gentlemen!' he shouted. 'The captain has estimated the day's run ending midday tomorrow, at five hundred and fifteen miles. As usual we will take the ten numbers on either side of it to make up the range. That makes it five hundred and five to five hundred and twenty-five. And of course for those who think the true figure
25 will be still farther away, there'll be "low field" and "high field" sold separately as well. Now, we'll draw the first numbers out of the hat . . . here we are . . . five hundred and twelve?'
   The room became quiet. The people sat still in their chairs, all eyes watching the auctioneer. There was a certain tension in the air,
30 and as the bids got higher, the tension grew. This wasn't a game or a joke; you could be sure of that by the way one man would look across at another who had raised his bid – smiling perhaps, but only the lips smiling, the eyes bright and absolutely cold.
   Number five hundred and twelve was knocked down for one
35 hundred and ten pounds. The next three or four numbers fetched roughly the same amount.

The ship was rolling heavily, and each time she went over, the wooden panelling on the walls creaked as if it were going to split. The passengers held on to the arms of their chairs, concentrating upon the auction.

'Low field!' the auctioneer called out. 'The next number is low  5 field.'

Mr Botibol sat up very straight and tense. He would wait, he had decided, until the others had finished bidding, then he would jump in and make the last bid. He had figured that there must be at least five hundred dollars in his account at the bank at home,  10 probably nearer six. That was about two hundred pounds – over two hundred. This ticket wouldn't fetch more than that.

'As you all know,' the auctioneer was saying, 'low field covers every number *below* the smallest number in the range, in this case every number below five hundred and five. So, if you think this  15 ship is going to cover less than five hundred and five miles in the twenty-four hours ending at noon tomorrow, you better get in and buy this number. So what am I bid?'

It went clear up to one hundred and thirty pounds. Others beside Mr Botibol seemed to have noticed that the weather was rough.  20 One hundred and forty . . . fifty . . . There it stopped. The auctioneer raised his hammer.

'Going at one hundred and fifty . . .'

'Sixty!' Mr Botibol called, and every face in the room turned and looked at him.  25

'Seventy!'

'Eighty!' Mr Botibol called.

'Ninety!'

'Two hundred!' Mr Botibol called. He wasn't stopping now – not for anyone.  30

There was a pause.

'Any advance on two hundred pounds?'

Sit still, he told himself. Sit absolutely still and don't look up. It's unlucky to look up. Hold your breath. No one's going to bid you up so long as you hold your breath.  35

'Going for two hundred pounds . . .' The auctioneer had a pink

bald head and there were little beads of sweat sparkling on top of it. 'Going . . .' Mr Botibol held his breath. 'Going . . . Gone!' The man banged the hammer on the table. Mr Botibol wrote out a cheque and handed it to the auctioneer's assistant, then he settled
5 back in his chair to wait for the finish. He did not want to go to bed before he knew how much there was in the pool.

They added it up after the last number had been sold and it came to twenty-one hundred-odd pounds. That was around six thousand dollars. Ninety per cent to go to the winner, ten per cent to seamen's
10 charities. Ninety per cent of six thousand was five thousand four hundred. Well – that was enough. He could buy the Lincoln convertible and there would be something left over, too. With this gratifying thought he went off, happy and excited, to his cabin.

When Mr Botibol awoke the next morning he lay quite still for
15 several minutes with his eyes shut, listening for the sound of the gale, waiting for the roll of the ship. There was no sound of any gale and the ship was not rolling. He jumped up and peered out of the porthole. The sea – Oh Jesus God – was smooth as glass, the great ship was moving through it fast, obviously making up for
20 time lost during the night. Mr Botibol turned away and sat slowly down on the edge of his bunk. A fine electricity of fear was beginning to prickle under the skin of his stomach. He hadn't a hope now. One of the higher numbers was certain to win it after this.

'Oh, my God,' he said aloud. 'What shall I do?'

25 What, for example, would Ethel say? It was simply not possible to tell her he had spent almost all of their two years' savings on a ticket in the ship's pool. Nor was it possible to keep the matter secret. To do that he would have to tell her to stop drawing cheques. And what about the monthly instalments on the television set and
30 the *Encyclopaedia Britannica*? Already he could see the anger and contempt in the woman's eyes, the blue becoming grey and the eyes themselves narrowing as they always did when there was anger in them.

'Oh, my God. What *shall* I do?'

35 There was no point in pretending that he had the slightest chance now – not unless the goddam ship started to go backwards. They'd

have to put her in reverse and go full speed astern and keep right
on going if he was to have any chance of winning it now. Well,
maybe he should ask the captain to do just that. Offer him ten per
cent of the profits. Offer him more if he wanted it. Mr Botibol
started to giggle. Then very suddenly he stopped, his eyes and      5
mouth both opening wide in a kind of shocked surprise. For it was
at this moment that the idea came. It hit him hard and quick, and
he jumped up from the bed, terribly excited, ran over to the porthole
and looked out again. Well, he thought, why not? Why ever not?
The sea was calm and he wouldn't have any trouble keeping afloat   10
until they picked him up. He had a vague feeling that someone
had done this thing before, but that didn't prevent him from doing
it again. The ship would have to stop and lower a boat, and the
boat would have to go back maybe half a mile to get him, and then
it would have to return to the ship, the whole thing. An hour was  15
about thirty miles. It would knock thirty miles off the day's run.
That would do it. 'Low field' would be sure to win it then. Just so
long as he made certain someone saw him falling over; but that
would be simple to arrange. And he'd better wear light clothes,
something easy to swim in. Sports clothes, that was it. He would   20
dress as though he were going up to play some deck tennis – just
a shirt and a pair of shorts and tennis shoes. And leave his watch
behind. What was the time? Nine-fifteen. The sooner the better,
then. Do it now and get it over with. Have to do it soon, because
the time limit was midday.                                         25

Mr Botibol was both frightened and excited when he stepped
out on to the sun deck in his sports clothes. His small body was
wide at the hips, tapering upward to extremely narrow sloping
shoulders, so that it resembled, in shape at any rate, a bollard. His
white skinny legs were covered with black hairs, and he came      30
cautiously out on deck, treading softly in his tennis shoes. Nervously
he looked around him. There was only one other person in sight,
an elderly woman with very thick ankles and immense buttocks
who was leaning over the rail staring at the sea. She was wearing
a coat of Persian lamb and the collar was turned up so Mr Botibol  35
couldn't see her face.

He stood still, examining her carefully from a distance. Yes, he told himself, she would probably do. She would probably give the alarm just as quickly as anyone else. But wait one minute, take your time, William Botibol, take your time. Remember what you
5 told yourself a few minutes ago in the cabin when you were changing? You remember that?

The thought of leaping off a ship into the ocean a thousand miles from the nearest land had made Mr Botibol – a cautious man at the best of times – unusually advertent. He was by no means
10 satisfied yet that this woman he saw before him was *absolutely certain* to give the alarm when he made his jump. In his opinion there were two possible reasons why she might fail him. Firstly, she might be deaf and blind. It was not very probable, but on the other hand it *might* be so, and why take a chance? All he had to do
15 was check it by talking to her for a moment beforehand. Secondly – and this will demonstrate how suspicious the mind of a man can become when it is working through self-preservation and fear – secondly, it had occurred to him that the woman might herself be the owner of one of the high numbers in the pool and as such
20 would have a sound financial reason for not wishing to stop the ship. Mr Botibol recalled that people had killed their fellows for far less than six thousand dollars. It was happening every day in the newspapers. So why take a chance on that either? Check on it first. Be sure of your facts. Find out about it by a little polite
25 conversation. Then, provided that the woman appeared also to be a pleasant, kindly human being, the thing was a cinch and he could leap overboard with a light heart.

Mr Botibol advanced casually towards the woman and took up a position beside her, leaning on the rail. 'Hullo,' he said pleasantly.
30 She turned and smiled at him, a surprisingly lovely, almost a beautiful smile, although the face itself was very plain. 'Hullo,' she answered him.

Check, Mr Botibol told himself, on the first question. She is neither blind nor deaf. 'Tell me,' he said, coming straight to the
35 point, 'what did you think of the auction last night?'

'Auction?' she said, frowning. 'Auction? What auction?'

'You know, that silly old thing they have in the lounge after dinner, selling numbers on the ship's daily run. I just wondered what you thought about it.'

She shook her head, and again she smiled, a sweet and pleasant smile that had in it perhaps the trace of an apology. 'I'm very lazy,' she said. 'I always go to bed early. I have my dinner in bed. It's so restful to have dinner in bed.'

Mr Botibol smiled back at her and began to edge away. 'Got to go and get my exercise now,' he said. 'Never miss my exercise in the morning. It was nice seeing you. Very nice seeing you . . .' He retreated about ten paces, and the woman let him go without looking around.

Everything was now in order. The sea was calm, he was lightly dressed for swimming, there were almost certainly no man-eating sharks in this part of the Atlantic, and there was this pleasant kindly old woman to give the alarm. It was a question now only of whether the ship would be delayed long enough to swing the balance in his favour. Almost certainly it would. In any event, he could do a little to help in that direction himself. He could make a few difficulties about getting hauled up into the lifeboat. Swim around a bit, back away from them surreptitiously as they tried to come up close to fish him out. Every minute, every second gained would help him win. He began to move forward again to the rail, but now a new fear assailed him. Would he get caught in the propeller? He had heard about that happening to persons falling off the sides of big ships. But then, he wasn't going to fall, he was going to jump, and that was a very different thing. Provided he jumped out far enough he would be sure to clear the propeller.

Mr Botibol advanced slowly to a position at the rail about twenty yards away from the woman. She wasn't looking at him now. So much the better. He didn't want her watching him as he jumped off. So long as no one was watching he would be able to say afterwards that he had slipped and fallen by accident. He peered over the side of the ship. It was a long, long drop. Come to think of it now, he might easily hurt himself badly if he hit the water flat. Wasn't there someone who once split his stomach open that way,

doing a belly flop from the high dive? He must jump straight and land feet first. Go in like a knife. Yes, sir. The water seemed cold and deep and grey and it made him shiver to look at it. But it was now or never. Be a man, William Botibol, be a man. All right then
5 ... now ... here goes ...

He climbed up on to the wide wooden top-rail, stood there poised, balancing for three terrifying seconds, then he leaped – he leaped up and out as far as he could go and at the same time he shouted '*Help!*'
10 '*Help! Help!*' he shouted as he fell. Then he hit the water and went under.

When the first shout for help sounded, the woman who was leaning on the rail started up and gave a little jump of surprise. She looked around quickly and saw sailing past her through the
15 air this small man dressed in white shorts and tennis shoes, spread-eagled and shouting as he went. For a moment she looked as though she weren't quite sure what she ought to do: throw a lifebelt, run away and give the alarm, or simply turn and yell. She drew back a pace from the rail and swung half around facing up to the
20 bridge, and for this brief moment she remained motionless, tense, undecided. Then almost at once she seemed to relax, and she leaned forward far over the rail, staring at the water where it was turbulent in the ship's wake. Soon a tiny round black head appeared in the foam, an arm raised above it, once, twice, vigorously waving,
25 and a small faraway voice was heard calling something that was difficult to understand. The woman leaned still farther over the rail, trying to keep the little bobbing black speck in sight, but soon, so very soon, it was such a long way away that she couldn't even be sure it was there at all.
30 After a while another woman came out on deck. This one was bony and angular, and she wore horn-rimmed spectacles. She spotted the first woman and walked over to her, treading the deck in the deliberate, military fashion of all spinsters.

'So *there* you are,' she said.
35 The woman with the fat ankles turned and looked at her, but said nothing.

'I've been searching for you,' the bony one continued. 'Searching all over.'

'It's very odd,' the woman with the fat ankles said. 'A man dived overboard just now, with his clothes on.'

'Nonsense!'

'Oh yes. He said he wanted to get some exercise and he dived in and didn't even bother to take his clothes off.'

'You better come down now,' the bony woman said. Her mouth had suddenly become firm, her whole face sharp and alert, and she spoke less kindly than before. 'And don't you ever go wandering about on deck alone like this again. You know quite well you're meant to wait for me.'

'Yes, Maggie,' the woman with the fat ankles answered, and again she smiled, a tender, trusting smile, and she took the hand of the other one and allowed herself to be led away across the deck.

'Such a nice man,' she said. 'He waved to me.'

# The Butler

As soon as George Cleaver had made his first million, he and Mrs
Cleaver moved out of their small suburban villa into an elegant
London house. They acquired a French chef called Monsieur
Estragon and an English butler called Tibbs, both wildly expensive.
5 With the help of these two experts, the Cleavers set out to climb
the social ladder and began to give dinner parties several times a
week on a lavish scale.

But these dinners never seemed quite to come off. There was
no animation, no spark to set the conversation alight, no style at
10 all. Yet the food was superb and the service faultless.

'What the heck's wrong with our parties, Tibbs?' Mr Cleaver
said to the butler. 'Why don't nobody never loosen up and let
themselves go?'

Tibbs inclined his head to one side and looked at the ceiling. 'I
15 hope, sir, you will not be offended if I offer a small suggestion.'

'What is it?'

'It's the wine, sir.'

'What about the wine?'

'Well, sir, Monsieur Estragon serves superb food. Superb food
20 should be accompanied by superb wine. But you serve them a
cheap and very odious Spanish red.'

'Then why in heaven's name didn't you say so before, you twit?'
cried Mr Cleaver. 'I'm not short of money. I'll give them the best
flipping wine in the world if that's what they want! What *is* the best
25 wine in the world?'

'Claret, sir,' the butler replied, 'from the greatest *châteaux* in
Bordeaux – Lafite, Latour, Haut-Brion, Margaux, Mouton-

Rothschild and Cheval Blanc. And from only the very greatest
vintage years, which are, in my opinion, 1906, 1914, 1929 and
1945. Cheval Blanc was also magnificent in 1895 and 1921, and
Haut-Brion in 1906.'

'Buy them all!' said Mr Cleaver. 'Fill the flipping cellar from top   5
to bottom!'

'I can try, sir,' the butler said. 'But wines like these are extremely
rare and cost a fortune.'

'I don't give a hoot what they cost!' said Mr Cleaver. 'Just go
out and get them!'   10

That was easier said than done. Nowhere in England or in France
could Tibbs find any wine from 1895, 1906, 1914 or 1921. But he
did manage to get hold of some twenty-nines and forty-fives. The
bills for these wines were astronomical. They were in fact so
huge that even Mr Cleaver began to sit up and take notice. And   15
his interest quickly turned into outright enthusiasm when the
butler suggested to him that a knowledge of wine was a very
considerable social asset. Mr Cleaver bought books on the subject
and read them from cover to cover. He also learned a great deal
from Tibbs himself, who taught him, among other things, just how   20
wine should be properly tasted. 'First, sir, you sniff it long and
deep, with your nose right inside the top of the glass, like this.
Then you take a mouthful and you open your lips a tiny bit and
suck in air, letting the air bubble through the wine. Watch me do
it. Then you roll it vigorously around your mouth. And finally you   25
swallow it.'

In due course, Mr Cleaver came to regard himself as an expert
on wine, and inevitably he turned into a colossal bore. 'Ladies and
gentlemen,' he would announce at dinner, holding up his glass,
'this is a Margaux '29! The greatest year of the century! Fantastic   30
bouquet! Smells of cowslips! And notice especially the after taste
and how the tiny trace of tannin gives it that glorious astringent
quality! Terrific, ain't it?'

The guests would nod and sip and mumble a few praises, but
that was all.   35

'What's the matter with the silly twerps?' Mr Cleaver said to

Tibbs after this had gone on for some time. 'Don't none of them appreciate a great wine?'

The butler laid his head to one side and gazed upward. 'I think they *would* appreciate it, sir,' he said, 'if they were able to taste it.
5 But they can't.'

'What the heck d'you mean, they can't taste it?'

'I believe, sir, that you have instructed Monsieur Estragon to put liberal quantities of vinegar in the salad-dressing.'

'What's wrong with that? I like vinegar.'

10 'Vinegar,' the butler said, 'is the enemy of wine. It destroys the palate. The dressing should be made of pure olive oil and a little lemon juice. Nothing else.'

'Hogwash!' said Mr Cleaver.

'As you wish, sir.'

15 'I'll say it again, Tibbs. You're talking hogwash. The vinegar don't spoil my palate one bit.'

'You are very fortunate, sir,' the butler murmured, backing out of the room.

That night at dinner, the host began to mock his butler in front
20 of the guests. 'Mister Tibbs,' he said, 'has been trying to tell me I can't taste my wine if I put vinegar in the salad-dressing. Right, Tibbs?'

'Yes, sir,' Tibbs replied gravely.

'And I told him hogwash. Didn't I, Tibbs?'

25 'Yes, sir.'

'This wine,' Mr Cleaver went on, raising his glass, 'tastes to me exactly like a Château Lafite '45, and what's more it is a Château Lafite '45.'

Tibbs, the butler, stood very still and erect near the sideboard,
30 his face pale. 'If you'll forgive me, sir,' he said, 'that is not a Lafite '45.'

Mr Cleaver swung round in his chair and stared at the butler. 'What the heck d'you mean,' he said. 'There's the empty bottles beside you to prove it!'

35 These great clarets, being old and full of sediment, were always decanted by Tibbs before dinner. They were served in cut-glass

decanters, while the empty bottles, as is the custom, were placed on the sideboard. Right now, two empty bottles of Lafite '45 were standing on the sideboard for all to see.

'The wine you are drinking, sir,' the butler said quietly, 'happens to be that cheap and rather odious Spanish red.'

Mr Cleaver looked at the wine in his glass, then at the butler. The blood was coming to his face now, his skin was turning scarlet. 'You're lying, Tibbs!' he said.

'No sir, I'm not lying,' the butler said. 'As a matter of fact, I have never served you any other wine but Spanish red since I've been here. It seemed to suit you very well.'

'I don't believe him!' Mr Cleaver cried out to his guests. 'The man's gone mad.'

'Great wines,' the butler said, 'should be treated with reverence. It is bad enough to destroy the palate with three or four cocktails before dinner, as you people do, but when you slosh vinegar over your food into the bargain, then you might just as well be drinking dishwater.'

Ten outraged faces around the table stared at the butler. He had caught them off balance. They were speechless.

'This,' the butler said, reaching out and touching one of the empty bottles lovingly with his fingers, 'this is the last of the forty-fives. The twenty-nines have already been finished. But they were glorious wines. Monsieur Estragon and I enjoyed them immensely.'

The butler bowed and walked quite slowly from the room. He crossed the hall and went out of the front door of the house into the street where Monsieur Estragon was already loading their suitcases into the boot of the small car which they owned together.

# The Hitchhiker

🎧 I had a new car. It was an exciting toy, a big BMW 3.3 Li, which means 3.3 litre, long wheelbase, fuel injection. It had a top speed of 129 mph and terrific acceleration. The body was pale blue. The seats inside were darker blue and they were made of leather, genuine
5 soft leather of the finest quality. The windows were electrically operated and so was the sunroof. The radio aerial popped up when I switched on the radio, and disappeared when I switched it off. The powerful engine growled and grunted impatiently at slow speeds, but at sixty miles an hour the growling stopped and the
10 motor began to purr with pleasure.

I was driving up to London by myself. It was a lovely June day. They were haymaking in the fields and there were buttercups along both sides of the road. I was whispering along at 70 mph, leaning back comfortably in my seat, with no more than a couple of fingers
15 resting lightly on the wheel to keep her steady. Ahead of me I saw a man thumbing a lift. I touched the brake and brought the car to a stop beside him. I always stopped for hitchhikers. I knew just how it used to feel to be standing on the side of a country road watching the cars go by. I hated the drivers for pretending they
20 didn't see me, especially the ones in big empty cars with three empty seats. The large expensive cars seldom stopped. It was always the smaller ones that offered you a lift, or the rusty ones or the ones that were already crammed full of children and the driver would say, 'I think we can squeeze in one more.'

25 The hitchhiker poked his head through the open window and said, 'Going to London, guv'nor?'

'Yes,' I said. 'Jump in.'

He got in and I drove on.

He was a small ratty-faced man with grey teeth. His eyes were dark and quick and clever, like rat's eyes, and his ears were slightly pointed at the top. He had a cloth cap on his head and he was wearing a greyish-coloured jacket with enormous pockets. The grey jacket, together with the quick eyes and the pointed ears, made him look more than anything like some sort of huge human rat.

'What part of London are you headed for?' I asked him.

'I'm going right through London and out the other side,' he said. 'I'm goin' to Epsom, for the races. It's Derby Day today.'

'So it is,' I said. 'I wish I were going with you. I love betting on horses.'

'I never bet on horses,' he said. 'I don't even watch 'em run. That's a stupid silly business.'

'Then why do you go?' I asked.

He didn't seem to like that question. His ratty little face went absolutely blank and he sat there staring straight ahead at the road, saying nothing.

'I expect you help to work the betting machines or something like that,' I said.

'That's even sillier,' he answered. 'There's no fun working them lousy machines and selling tickets to mugs. Any fool could do that.'

There was a long silence. I decided not to question him any more. I remembered how irritated I used to get in my hitchhiking days when drivers kept asking *me* questions. Where are you going? Why are you going there? What's your job? Are you married? Do you have a girlfriend? What's her name? How old are you? And so forth and so forth. I used to hate it.

'I'm sorry,' I said. 'It's none of my business what you do. The trouble is I'm a writer, and most writers are terribly nosy.'

'You write books?' he asked.

'Yes.'

'Writin' books is okay,' he said. 'It's what I call a skilled trade. I'm in a skilled trade too. The folks I despise is them that spend all their lives doin' crummy old routine jobs with no skill in 'em at all. You see what I mean?'

'Yes.'

'The secret of life,' he said, 'is to become very very good at somethin' that's very very 'ard to do.'

'Like you,' I said.

5 'Exactly. You and me both.'

'What makes you think that *I'm* any good at my job?' I asked. 'There's an awful lot of bad writers around.'

'You wouldn't be drivin' about in a car like this if you weren't no good at it,' he answered. 'It must've cost a tidy packet, this little job.'

10 'It wasn't cheap.'

'What can she do flat out?' he asked.

'One hundred and twenty-nine miles an hour,' I told him.

'I'll bet she won't do it.'

'I'll bet she will.'

15 'All car-makers is liars,' he said. 'You can buy any car you like and it'll never do what the makers say it will in the ads.'

'This one will.'

'Open 'er up then and prove it,' he said. 'Go on guv'nor, open 'er up and let's see what she'll do.'

20 There is a traffic circle at Chalfont St Peter and immediately beyond there's a long straight section of divided highway. We came out of the circle onto the highway and I pressed my foot hard down on the accelerator. The big car leaped forward as though she'd been stung. In ten seconds or so, we were doing ninety.

25 'Lovely!' he cried. 'Beautiful! Keep goin'!'

I had the accelerator jammed down against the floor and I held it there.

'One hundred!' he shouted. 'A hundred and five! A hundred and ten! A hundred and fifteen! Go on! Don't slack off!'

30 I was in the outside lane and we flashed past several cars as though they were standing still – a green Mini, a big cream-coloured Citroen, a white Land Rover, a huge truck with a container on the back, an orange-coloured Volkswagen Minibus . . .

'A hundred and twenty!' my passenger shouted, jumping up and 35 down. 'Go on! Go on! Get 'er up to one-two-nine!'

At that moment, I heard the scream of a police siren. It was so loud it seemed to be right inside the car, and then a cop on a motorcycle loomed up alongside us in the inside lane and went past us and raised a hand for us to stop.

'Oh, my sainted aunt!' I said. 'That's torn it!'

The cop must have been doing about a hundred and thirty when  5
he passed us, and he took plenty of time slowing down. Finally, he pulled to the side of the road and I pulled in behind him. 'I didn't know police motorcycles could *go* as fast as that,' I said rather lamely.

'That one can,' my passenger said. 'It's the same make as yours.  10
It's a BMW R90S. Fastest bike on the road. That's what they're usin' nowadays.'

The cop got off his motorcycle and leaned the machine sideways onto its prop stand. Then he took off his gloves and placed them carefully on the seat. He was in no hurry now. He had us where  15
he wanted us and he knew it.

'This is real trouble,' I said. 'I don't like it one little bit.'

'Don't talk to 'im more than necessary, you understand,' my companion said. 'Just sit tight and keep mum.'

Like an executioner approaching his victim, the cop came strolling  20
slowly towards us. He was a big meaty man with a belly, and his blue breeches were skin-tight around enormous thighs. His goggles were pulled up onto the helmet, showing a smouldering red face with wide cheeks.

We sat there like guilty schoolboys, waiting for him to arrive.  25

'Watch out for this man,' my passenger whispered, ''e looks mean as the devil.'

The cop came round to my open window and placed one meaty hand on the sill. 'What's the hurry?' he said.

'No hurry, officer,' I answered.  30

'Perhaps there's a woman in the back having a baby and you're rushing her to hospital? Is that it?'

'No, officer.'

'Or perhaps your house is on fire and you're dashing home to rescue the family from upstairs?' His voice was dangerously soft  35
and mocking.

'My house isn't on fire, officer.'

'In that case,' he said, 'you've got yourself into a nasty mess, haven't you? Do you know what the speed limit is in this country?'

'Seventy,' I said.

5 'And do you mind telling me exactly what speed you were doing just now?'

I shrugged and didn't say anything.

When he spoke next, he raised his voice so loud that I jumped. '*One hundred and twenty miles per hour!*' he barked. 'That's *fifty*

10 miles an hour over the limit!'

He turned his head and spat out a big gob of spit. It landed on the wing of my car and started sliding down over my beautiful blue paint. Then he turned back again and stared hard at my passenger. 'And who are you?' he asked sharply.

15 'He's a hitchhiker,' I said. 'I'm giving him a lift.'

'I didn't ask you,' he said. 'I asked him.'

''Ave I done somethin' wrong?' my passenger asked. His voice was soft and oily as haircream.

'That's more than likely,' the cop answered. 'Anyway, you're a

20 witness. I'll deal with you in a minute. Driver's licence,' he snapped, holding out his hand.

I gave him my driver's licence.

He unbuttoned the left-hand breast pocket of his tunic and brought out the dreaded book of tickets. Carefully he copied the

25 name and address from my licence. Then he gave it back to me. He strolled around to the front of the car and read the number from the licence plate and wrote that down as well. He filled in the date, the time and the details of my offence. Then he tore out the top copy of the ticket. But before handing it to me, he checked

30 that all information had come through clearly on his own carbon copy. Finally, he replaced the book in his breast pocket and fastened the button.

'Now you,' he said to my passenger, and he walked around to the other side of the car. From the other breast pocket he produced

35 a small black notebook. 'Name?' he snapped.

'Michael Fish,' my passenger said.

'Address?'

'Fourteen, Windsor Lane, Luton.'

'Show me something to prove this is your real name and address,' the policeman said.

My passenger fished in his pockets and came out with a driver's licence of his own. The policeman checked the name and address and handed it back to him. 'What's your job?' he asked sharply.

'I'm an 'od carrier.'

'A *what?*'

'An 'od carrier.'

'Spell it.'

'H-o-d c-a–'

'That'll do. And what's a hod carrier, may I ask?'

'An 'od carrier, officer, is a person 'oo carries the cement up the ladder to the bricklayer. And the 'od is what 'ee carries it in. It's got a long 'andle, and on the top you've got bits of wood set at an angle . . .'

'All right, all right. Who's your employer?'

'Don't 'ave one. I'm unemployed.'

The cop wrote this down in the black notebook. Then he returned the book to his pocket and did up the button.

'When I get back to the station I'm going to do a little checking up on you,' he said to my passenger.

'Me? What've I done wrong?' the rat-faced man asked.

'I don't like your face, that's all,' the cop said. 'And we just might have a picture of it somewhere in our files.' He strolled round the car and returned to my window.

'I suppose you know you're in serious trouble,' he said to me.

'Yes, officer.'

'You won't be driving this fancy car of yours again for a very long time, not after *we've* finished with you. You won't be driving *any* car again, come to that, for several years. And a good thing, too. I hope they lock you up for a spell into the bargain.'

'You mean prison?' I asked, alarmed.

'Absolutely,' he said, smacking his lips. 'In the clink. Behind the

bars. Along with all the other criminals who break the law. *And* a
hefty fine into the bargain. Nobody will be more pleased about
that than me. I'll see you in court, both of you. You'll be getting
a summons to appear.'

5    He turned and walked over to his motorcycle. He flipped the
prop stand back into position with his foot and swung his leg over
the saddle. Then he kicked the starter and roared off up the road
out of sight.

'Phew!' I gasped. 'That's done it.'

10    'We was caught,' my passenger said. 'We was caught good and
proper.'

'I was caught, you mean.'

'That's right,' he said. 'What you goin' to do now, guv'nor?'

'I'm going straight up to London to talk to my solicitor,' I said.
15 I started my car and drove on.

'You mustn't believe what 'ee said to you about goin' to prison,'
my passenger said. 'They don't put somebody in the clink just for
speedin'.'

'Are you sure of that?' I asked.

20    'I'm positive,' he answered. 'They can take your licence away
and they can give you a whoppin' big fine, but that'll be the end
of it.'

I felt tremendously relieved.

'By the way,' I said, 'why did you lie to him?'

25    'Who, me?' he said. 'What makes you think I lied?'

'You told him you were an unemployed hod carrier. But you
told *me* you were in a highly skilled trade.'

'So I am,' he said. 'But it don't do to tell everythin' to a copper.'

'So what *do* you do?' I asked him.

30    'Ah,' he said slyly. 'That'd be tellin', wouldn't it?'

'Is it something you're ashamed of?'

'Ashamed?' he cried. 'Me, ashamed of my job? I'm about as
proud of it as anybody could be in the entire world!'

'Then why won't you tell me?'

35    'You writers really is nosy parkers, aren't you?' he said. 'And

you ain't goin' to be 'appy, I don't think, until you've found out exactly what the answer is?'

'I don't really care one way or the other,' I told him, lying.

He gave me a crafty look out of the sides of his eyes. 'I think you do care,' he said. 'I can see it in your face that you think I'm in some kind of very peculiar trade and you're just achin' to know what it is.'

I didn't like the way he read my thoughts. I kept quiet and stared at the road ahead.

'You'd be right, too,' he went on. 'I *am* in a very peculiar trade. I'm in the queerest peculiar trade of 'em all.'

I waited for him to go on.

'That's why I 'as to be extra careful 'oo I'm talking to, you see. 'Ow am I to know, for instance, you're not another copper in plain clothes?'

'Do I look like a copper?'

'No,' he said. 'You don't. And you ain't. Any fool could tell that.'

He took from his pocket a tin of tobacco and a packet of cigarette papers and started to roll a cigarette. I was watching him out of the corner of my eye, and the speed with which he performed this rather difficult operation was incredible. The cigarette was rolled and ready in about five seconds. He ran his tongue along the edge of the paper, stuck it down and popped the cigarette between his lips. Then, as if from nowhere, a lighter appeared in his hand. The lighter flamed. The cigarette was lit. The lighter disappeared. It was altogether a remarkable performance.

'I've never seen anyone roll a cigarette as fast as that,' I said.

'Ah,' he said, taking a deep suck of smoke. 'So you noticed.'

'Of course I noticed. It was quite fantastic.'

He sat back and smiled. It pleased him very much that I had noticed how quickly he could roll a cigarette. 'You want to know what makes me able to do it?' he asked.

'Go on then.'

'It's because I've got fantastic fingers. These fingers of mine,' he said, holding up both hands high in front of him, 'are

quicker and cleverer than the fingers of the best piano player in
the world!'

'Are you a piano player?'

'Don't be daft,' he said. 'Do I look like a piano player?'

5    I glanced at his fingers. They were so beautifully shaped, so slim
and long and elegant, they didn't seem to belong to the rest of
him at all. They looked like the fingers of a brain surgeon or a
watchmaker.

'My job,' he went on, 'is a hundred times more difficult than
10  playin' the piano. Any twerp can learn to do that. There's titchy
little kids learnin' to play the piano at almost any 'ouse you go into
these days. That's right, ain't it?'

'More or less,' I said.

'Of course it's right. But there's not one person in ten million
15  can learn to do what I do. Not one in ten million! 'Ow about that?'

'Amazing,' I said.

'You're darn right it's amazin',' he said.

'I think I know what you do,' I said. 'You do conjuring tricks.
You're a conjuror.'

20  'Me?' he snorted. 'A conjuror? Can you picture me goin' round
crummy kids' parties makin' rabbits come out of top 'ats?'

'Then you're a card player. You get people into card games and
you deal yourself out marvellous hands.'

'Me! A rotten cardsharper!' he cried. 'That's a miserable racket
25  if ever there was one.'

'All right. I give up.'

I was taking the car along slowly now, at no more than forty
miles an hour, to make sure I wasn't stopped again. We had come
onto the main London–Oxford road and were running down the
30  hill toward Denham.

Suddenly, my passenger was holding up a black leather belt in
his hand. 'Ever seen this before?' he asked. The belt had a brass
buckle of unusual design.

'Hey!' I said. 'That's mine, isn't it? It *is* mine! Where did you
35  get it?'

He grinned and waved the belt gently from side to side. 'Where d'you think I got it?' he said. 'Off the top of your trousers, of course.'

I reached down and felt for my belt. It was gone.

'You mean you took it off me while we've been driving along?' I asked flabbergasted.

He nodded, watching me all the time with those little black ratty eyes.

'That's impossible,' I said. 'You'd have had to undo the buckle and slide the whole thing out through the loops all the way round. I'd have seen you doing it. And even if I hadn't seen you, I'd have felt it.'

'Ah, but you didn't, did you?' he said, triumphant. He dropped the belt on his lap, and now all at once there was a brown shoelace dangling from his fingers. 'And what about this, then?' he exclaimed, waving the shoelace.

'What about it?' I said.

'Anyone around 'ere missing a shoelace?' he asked, grinning.

I glanced down at my shoes. The lace of one of them was missing. 'Good grief!' I said. 'How did you do that? I never saw you bending down.'

'You never saw nothin',' he said proudly. 'You never even saw me move an inch. And you know why?'

'Yes,' I said. 'Because you've got fantastic fingers.'

'Exactly right!' he cried. 'You catch on pretty quick, don't you?' He sat back and sucked away at his homemade cigarette, blowing the smoke out in a thin stream against the windshield. He knew he had impressed me greatly with those two tricks, and this made him very happy. 'I don't want to be late,' he said. 'What time is it?'

'There's a clock in front of you,' I told him.

'I don't trust car clocks,' he said. 'What does your watch say?'

I hitched up my sleeve to look at the watch on my wrist. It wasn't there. I looked at the man. He looked back at me, grinning.

'You've taken that, too,' I said.

He held out his hand and there was my watch lying in his palm. 'Nice bit of stuff, this,' he said. 'Superior quality. Eighteen-carat gold. Easy to sell, too. It's never any trouble gettin' rid of quality goods.'

'I'd like it back, if you don't mind,' I said rather huffily.

He placed the watch carefully on the leather tray in front of him.

5 'I wouldn't nick anything from you, guv'nor,' he said. 'You're my pal. You're givin' me a lift.'

'I'm glad to hear it,' I said.

'All I'm doin' is answerin' your question,' he went on. 'You asked me what I do for a livin' and I'm showin' you.'

10 'What else have you got of mine?'

He smiled again, and now he started to take from the pocket of his jacket one thing after another that belonged to me – my driver's licence, a key ring with four keys on it, some pound notes, a few coins, a letter from my publishers, my diary, a stubby old pencil,

15 a cigarette lighter and, last of all, a beautiful old sapphire ring with pearls around it belonging to my wife. I was taking the ring up to a jeweller in London because one of the pearls was missing.

'Now *there's* another lovely piece of goods,' he said, turning the ring over in his fingers. 'That's eighteenth century, if I'm not

20 mistaken, from the reign of King George the Third.'

'You're right,' I said, impressed. 'You're absolutely right.'

He put the ring on the leather tray with the other items.

'So you're a pickpocket,' I said.

'I don't like that word,' he answered. 'It's a coarse and vulgar

25 word. Pickpockets is coarse and vulgar people who only do easy little amateur jobs. They lift money from blind old ladies.'

'What do you call yourself, then?'

'Me? I'm a fingersmith. I'm a professional fingersmith.' He spoke the words solemnly and proudly, as though he were telling me he

30 was President of the Royal College of Surgeons or the Archbishop of Canterbury.

'I've never heard that word before,' I said. 'Did you invent it?'

'Of course I didn't invent it,' he replied. 'It's the name given to them who's risen to the very top of the profession. You've heard

35 of a goldsmith or a silversmith, for instance. They're experts with gold and silver. I'm an expert with my fingers, so I'm a fingersmith.'

'It must be an interesting job.'

'It's a marvellous job,' he answered. 'It's lovely.'

'And that's why you go to the races?'

'Race meetings is easy meat,' he said. 'You just stand around after the race, watchin' for the lucky ones to queue up and draw their money. And when you see someone collectin' a big bundle of notes, you simply follows after 'im and 'elps yourself. But don't get me wrong, guv'nor. I never takes nothin' from a loser. Nor from poor people neither. I only go after them as can afford it, the winners and the rich.'

'That's very thoughtful of you,' I said. 'How often do you get caught?'

'Caught?' he cried, disgusted. '*Me* get caught! It's only pick-pockets get caught. Fingersmiths never. Listen, I could take the false teeth out of your mouth if I wanted to and you wouldn't even catch me!'

'I don't have false teeth,' I said.

'I know you don't,' he answered. 'Otherwise I'd 'ave 'ad 'em out long ago!'

I believed him. Those long slim fingers of his seemed able to do anything.

We drove on for a while without talking.

'That policeman's going to check up on you pretty thoroughly,' I said. 'Doesn't that worry you a bit?'

'Nobody's checkin' up on me,' he said.

'Of course they are. He's got your name and address written down most carefully in his black book.'

The man gave me another of his sly ratty little smiles. 'Ah, he said. 'So 'ee 'as. But I'll bet 'ee ain't got it all written down in 'is memory as well. I've never known a copper yet with a decent memory. Some of 'em can't even remember their own names.'

'What's memory got to do with it?' I asked. 'It's written down in his book, isn't it?'

'Yes, guv'nor, it is. But the trouble is, 'ee's lost the book. 'Ee's lost both books, the one with my name on it *and* the one with yours.'

In the long delicate fingers of his right hand, the man was holding up in triumph the two books he had taken from the policeman's pockets. 'Easiest job I ever done,' he announced proudly.

I nearly swerved the car into a milk truck, I was so excited.

5    'That copper's got nothin' on either of us now,' he said.

'You're a genius!' I cried.

''Ee's got no names, no addresses, no car number, no nothin',' he said.

'You're brilliant!'

10    'I think you'd better pull off this main road as soon as possible,' he said. 'Then we'd better build a little bonfire and burn these books.'

'You're a fantastic fellow!' I exclaimed.

'Thank you, guv'nor,' he said. 'It's always nice to be appreciated.'

# Mr Botibol

Mr Botibol pushed his way through the revolving doors and
emerged into the large foyer of the hotel. He took off his hat, and
holding it in front of him with both hands, he advanced nervously
a few paces, paused and stood looking around him, searching the
faces of the lunchtime crowd. Several people turned and stared at
him in mild astonishment, and he heard – or he thought he heard
– at least one woman's voice saying, 'My dear, *do* look what's just
come in!'

At last he spotted Mr Clements sitting at a small table in the far
corner, and he hurried over to him. Clements had seen him coming,
and now, as he watched Mr Botibol threading his way cautiously
between the tables and the people, walking on his toes in such a
meek and self-effacing manner and clutching his hat before him
with both hands, he thought how wretched it must be for any man
to look as conspicuous and as odd as this Botibol. He resembled,
to an extraordinary degree, an asparagus. His long narrow stalk
did not appear to have any shoulders at all; it merely tapered
upwards, growing gradually narrower and narrower until it came
to a kind of point at the top of the small bald head. He was tightly
encased in a shiny blue double-breasted suit, and this, for some
curious reason, accentuated the illusion of a vegetable to a preposterous degree.

Clements stood up, they shook hands, and then at once, even
before they had sat down again, Mr Botibol said, 'I have decided,
yes I have decided to accept the offer which you made to me before
you left my office last night.'

For some days Clements had been negotiating, on behalf of

clients, for the purchase of the firm known as Botibol & Co., of
which Mr Botibol was sole owner, and the night before, Clements
had made his first offer. This was merely an exploratory, much-too-
low bid, a kind of signal to the seller that the buyers were seriously
5 interested. And by God, thought Clements, the poor fool has gone
and accepted it. He nodded gravely many times in an effort to hide
his astonishment, and he said, 'Good, good. I'm so glad to hear
that, Mr Botibol.' Then he signalled a waiter and said, 'Two large
martinis.'

10 'No, please!' Mr Botibol lifted both hands in horrified protest.

'Come on,' Clements said. 'This is an occasion.'

'I drink very little, and never, no never during the middle of the
day.'

But Clements was in a gay mood now and he took no notice.
15 He ordered the martinis and when they came along Mr Botibol
was forced, by the banter and good humour of the other, to drink
to the deal which had just been concluded. Clements then spoke
briefly about the drawing up and signing of documents, and when
all that had been arranged, he called for two more cocktails. Again
20 Mr Botibol protested, but not quite so vigorously this time, and
Clements ordered the drinks and then he turned and smiled at the
other man in a friendly way. 'Well, Mr Botibol,' he said, 'now that
it's all over, I suggest we have a pleasant non-business lunch
together. What d'you say to that? And it's on me.'

25 'As you wish, as you wish,' Mr Botibol answered without any
enthusiasm. He had a small melancholy voice and a way of pro-
nouncing each word separately and slowly, as though he was
explaining something to a child.

When they went into the dining-room Clements ordered a bottle
30 of Lafite 1912 and a couple of plump roast partridges to go with
it. He had already calculated in his head the amount of his commission and he was feeling fine. He began to make bright conversation, switching smoothly from one subject to another in the hope
of touching on something that might interest his guest. But it was
35 no good. Mr Botibol appeared to be only half listening. Every now
and then he inclined his small bald head a little to one side or the

other and said, 'Indeed.' When the wine came along Clements tried to have a talk about that.

'I am sure it is excellent,' Mr Botibol said, 'but please give me only a drop.'

Clements told a funny story. When it was over, Mr Botibol regarded him solemnly for a few moments, then he said, 'How amusing.' After that Clements kept his mouth shut and they ate in silence. Mr Botibol was drinking his wine and he didn't seem to object when his host reached over and refilled his glass. By the time they had finished eating, Clements estimated privately that his guest had consumed at least three-quarters of the bottle.

'A cigar, Mr Botibol?'

'Oh no, thank you.'

'A little brandy?'

'No really. I am not accustomed . . .' Clements noticed that the man's cheeks were slightly flushed and that his eyes had become bright and watery. Might as well get the old boy properly drunk while I'm about it, he thought, and to the waiter he said, 'Two brandies.'

When the brandies arrived, Mr Botibol looked at his large glass suspiciously for a while, then he picked it up, took one quick birdlike sip and put it down again. 'Mr Clements,' he said suddenly, 'how I envy you.'

'Me? But why?'

'I will tell you, Mr Clements, I will tell you, if I may make so bold.' There was a nervous, mouselike quality in his voice which made it seem he was apologizing for everything he said.

'Please tell me,' Clements said.

'It is because to me you appear to have made such a success of your life.'

He's going to get melancholy drunk, Clements thought. He's one of the ones that gets melancholy and I can't stand it. 'Success,' he said. 'I don't see anything especially successful about me.'

'Oh yes, indeed. Your whole life, if I may say so, Mr Clements, appears to be such a pleasant and successful thing.'

'I'm a very ordinary person,' Clements said. He was trying to figure just how drunk the other really was.

'I believe,' said Mr Botibol, speaking slowly, separating each word carefully from the other, 'I believe that the wine has gone a
5  little to my head, but . . .' He paused, searching for words. '. . . But I do want to ask you just one question.' He had poured some salt on to the tablecloth and he was shaping it into a little mountain with the tip of one finger.

'Mr Clements,' he said without looking up, 'do you think that
10  it is possible for a man to live to the age of fifty-two without ever during his whole life having experienced one single small success in anything that he has done?'

'My dear Mr Botibol,' Clements laughed, 'everyone has his little successes from time to time, however small they may be.'

15  'Oh no,' Mr Botibol said gently. 'You are wrong. I, for example, cannot remember having had a single success of any sort during my whole life.'

'Now come!' Clements said, smiling. 'That can't be true. Why only this morning you sold your business for a hundred thousand.
20  I call that one hell of a success.'

'The business was left me by my father. When he died nine years ago, it was worth four times as much. Under my direction it has lost three-quarters of its value. You can hardly call that a success.'

Clements knew this was true. 'Yes, yes, all right,' he said. 'That
25  may be so, but all the same you know as well as I do that every man alive has his quota of little successes. Not big ones maybe. But lots of little ones. I mean, after all, goddammit, even scoring a goal at school was a little success, a little triumph, at the time; or making some runs or learning to swim. One forgets about them,
30  that's all. One just forgets.'

'I never scored a goal,' Mr Botibol said. 'And I never learned to swim.'

Clements threw up his hands and made exasperated noises. 'Yes yes, I know, but don't you see, don't you see there are thousands,
35  literally thousands of other things like . . . well . . . like catching a good fish, or fixing the motor of the car, or pleasing someone with

a present, or growing a decent row of French beans, or winning a little bet or . . . or . . . why hell, one can go on listing them for ever!'

'Perhaps *you* can, Mr Clements, but to the best of my knowledge, I have never done any of those things. That is what I am trying to tell you.'                                                                              5

Clements put down his brandy glass and stared with new interest at the remarkable shoulderless person who sat facing him. He was annoyed and he didn't feel in the least sympathetic. The man didn't inspire sympathy. He was a fool. He must be a fool. A tremendous    10 and absolute fool. Clements had a sudden desire to embarrass the man as much as he could. 'What about women, Mr Botibol?' There was no apology for the question in the tone of his voice.

'Women?'

'Yes women! Every man under the sun, even the most wretched    15 filthy down-and-out tramp, has some time or other had some sort of silly little success with . . .'

'Never!' cried Mr Botibol with sudden vigour. 'No sir, never!'

I'm going to hit him, Clements told himself. I can't stand this any longer and if I'm not careful I'm going to jump right up and    20 hit him. 'You mean you don't like them?' he said.

'Oh dear me yes, of course I like them. As a matter of fact I admire them very much, very much indeed. But I'm afraid . . . oh dear me . . . I do not know how to say it . . . I am afraid that I do not seem to get along with them very well. I never have. Never.    25 You see, Mr Clements, I *look* queer. I know I do. They stare at me, and often I see them laughing at me. I have never been able to get within . . . well, within striking distance of them, as you might say.' The trace of a smile, weak and infinitely sad, flickered around the corners of his mouth.                                            30

Clements had had enough. He mumbled something about how he was sure Mr Botibol was exaggerating the situation, then he glanced at his watch, called for the bill, and he said he was sorry but he would have to get back to the office.

They parted in the street outside the hotel and Mr Botibol took    35 a cab back to his house. He opened the front door, went into the

living-room and switched on the radio; then he sat down in a large leather chair, leaned back and closed his eyes. He didn't feel exactly giddy, but there was a singing in his ears and his thoughts were coming and going more quickly than usual. That solicitor gave me
5 too much wine, he told himself. I'll stay here for a while and listen to some music and I expect I'll go to sleep and after that I'll feel better.

They were playing a symphony on the radio. Mr Botibol had always been a casual listener to symphony concerts and he knew
10 enough to identify this as one of Beethoven's. But now, as he lay back in his chair listening to the marvellous music, a new thought began to expand slowly within his tipsy mind. It wasn't a dream because he was not asleep. It was a clear conscious thought and it was this: I am the composer of this music. I am a great composer.
15 This is my latest symphony and this is the first performance. The huge hall is packed with people – critics, musicians and music-lovers from all over the country – and I am up there in front of the orchestra, conducting.

Mr Botibol could see the whole thing. He could see himself up
20 on the rostrum dressed in a white tie and tails, and before him was the orchestra, the massed violins on his left, the violas in front, the cellos on his right, and back of them were all the woodwinds and bassoons and drums and cymbals, the players watching every movement of his baton with an intense, almost a fanatical reverence.
25 Behind him, in the half-darkness of the huge hall, was row upon row of white enraptured faces, looking up towards him, listening with growing excitement as yet another new symphony by the greatest composer the world has ever seen unfolded itself majestic-ally before them. Some of the audience were clenching their fists
30 and digging their nails into the palms of their hands because the music was so beautiful that they could hardly stand it. Mr Botibol became so carried away by this exciting vision that he began to swing his arms in time with the music in the manner of a conductor. He found it was such fun doing this that he decided to stand
35 up, facing the radio, in order to give himself more freedom of movement.

He stood there in the middle of the room, tall, thin and shoulderless, dressed in his tight blue double-breasted suit, his small
bald head jerking from side to side as he waved his arms in the air.
He knew the symphony well enough to be able occasionally to
anticipate changes in tempo or volume, and when the music became 5
loud and fast he beat the air so vigorously that he nearly knocked
himself over, when it was soft and hushed, he leaned forward to
quieten the players with gentle movements of his outstretched
hands, and all the time he could feel the presence of the huge
audience behind him, tense, immobile, listening. When at last 10
the symphony swelled to its tremendous conclusion, Mr Botibol
became more frenzied than ever and his face seemed to thrust itself
round to one side in an agony of effort as he tried to force more
and still more power from his orchestra during those final mighty
chords. 15

Then it was over. The announcer was saying something, but Mr
Botibol quickly switched off the radio and collapsed into his chair,
blowing heavily.

'Phew!' he said aloud. 'My goodness gracious me, what *have* I
been doing!' Small globules of sweat were oozing out all over his 20
face and forehead, trickling down his neck inside his collar. He
pulled out a handkerchief and wiped them away, and he lay there
for a while, panting, exhausted, but exceedingly exhilarated.

'Well, I must say,' he gasped, still speaking aloud, 'that *was* fun.
I don't know that I have ever had such fun before in all my life. 25
My goodness, it *was* fun, it really *was*!' Almost at once he began
to play with the idea of doing it again. But should he? Should he
allow himself to do it again? There was no denying that now, in
retrospect, he felt a little guilty about the whole business, and soon
he began to wonder whether there wasn't something downright 30
immoral about it all. Letting himself go like that! And imagining
he was a genius! It was wrong. He was sure other people didn't do
it. And what if Mason had come in the middle and seen him at it!
That would have been terrible!

He reached for the paper and pretended to read it, but soon 35
he was searching furtively among the radio programmes for the

evening. He put his finger under a line which said '8.30 Symphony Concert. Brahms Symphony No. 2'. He stared at it for a long time. The letters in the word 'Brahms' began to blur and recede, and gradually they disappeared altogether and were replaced by letters
5 which spelt 'Botibol'. Botibol's Symphony No. 2. It was printed quite clearly. He was reading it now, this moment. 'Yes, yes,' he whispered. 'First performance. The world is waiting to hear it. Will it be as great, they are asking, will it perhaps be greater than his earlier work? And the composer himself had been persuaded to
10 conduct. He is shy and retiring, hardly ever appears in public, but on this occasion he has been persuaded . . .'

Mr Botibol leaned forward in his chair and pressed the bell beside the fireplace. Mason, the butler, the only other person in the house, ancient, small and grave, appeared at the door.
15 'Er . . . Mason, have we any wine in the house?'

'Wine, sir?'

'Yes, wine.'

'Oh no, sir. We haven't had any wine this fifteen or sixteen years. Your father, sir . . .'
20 'I know, Mason, I know, but will you get some please. I want a bottle with my dinner.'

The butler was shaken. 'Very well, sir, and what shall it be?'

'Claret, Mason. The best you can obtain. Get a case. Tell them to send it round at once.'
25 When he was alone again, he was momentarily appalled by the simple manner in which he had made his decision. Wine for dinner! Just like that! Well, yes, why not? Why ever not now he came to think of it? He was his own master. And anyway it was essential that he have wine. It seemed to have a good effect, a very good
30 effect indeed. He wanted it and he was going to have it and to hell with Mason.

He rested for the remainder of the afternoon, and at seven-thirty Mason announced dinner. The bottle of wine was on the table and he began to drink it. He didn't give a damn about the way Mason
35 watched him as he refilled his glass. Three times he refilled it; then he left the table saying that he was not to be disturbed and returned

to the living-room. There was quarter of an hour to wait. He could think of nothing now except the coming concert. He lay back in the chair and allowed his thoughts to wander deliciously towards eight-thirty. He was the great composer waiting impatiently in his dressing-room in the concert-hall. He could hear in the distance the murmur of excitement from the crowd as they settled themselves in their seats. He knew what they were saying to each other. Same sort of thing the newspapers had been saying for months. Botibol is a genius, greater, far greater than Beethoven or Bach or Brahms or Mozart or any of them. Each new work of his is more magnificent than the last. What will the next one be like? We can hardly wait to hear it! Oh yes, he knew what they were saying. He stood up and began to pace the room. It was nearly time now. He seized a pencil from the table to use as a baton, then he switched on the radio. The announcer had just finished the preliminaries and suddenly there was a burst of applause which meant that the conductor was coming on to the platform. The previous concert in the afternoon had been from gramophone records, but this one was the real thing. Mr Botibol turned around, faced the fireplace and bowed graciously from the waist. Then he turned back to the radio and lifted his baton. The clapping stopped. There was a moment's silence. Someone in the audience coughed. Mr Botibol waited. The symphony began.

Once again, as he began to conduct, he could see clearly before him the whole orchestra and the faces of the players and even the expressions on their faces. Three of the violinists had grey hair. One of the cellists was very fat, another wore heavy brown-rimmed glasses, and there was a man in the second row playing a horn who had a twitch on one side of his face. But they were all magnificent. And so was the music. During certain impressive passages Mr Botibol experienced a feeling of exultation so powerful that it made him cry out for joy, and once during the Third Movement, a little shiver of ecstasy radiated spontaneously from his solar plexus and moved downward over the skin of his stomach like needles. But the thunderous applause and the cheering which came at the end of the symphony was the most splendid thing of all. He turned

slowly towards the fireplace and bowed. The clapping continued
and he went on bowing until at last the noise died away and the
announcer's voice jerked him suddenly back into the living-room.
He switched off the radio and collapsed into his chair, exhausted
5 but very happy.

As he lay there, smiling with pleasure, wiping his wet face, panting
for breath, he was already making plans for his next performance.
But why not do it properly? Why not convert one of the rooms into
a sort of concert-hall and have a stage and row of chairs and do
10 the thing properly? And have a gramophone so that one could
perform at any time without having to rely on the radio programme.
Yes by heavens, he would do it!

The next morning Mr Botibol arranged with a firm of decorators
that the largest room in the house be converted into a miniature
15 concert-hall. There was to be a raised stage at one end and the rest
of the floor-space was to be filled with rows of red plush seats. 'I'm
going to have some little concerts here,' he told the man from the
firm, and the man nodded and said that would be very nice. At
the same time he ordered a radio shop to instal an expensive
20 self-changing gramophone with two powerful amplifiers, one on
the stage, the other at the back of the auditorium. When he had done
this, he went off and bought all of Beethoven's nine symphonies
on gramophone records, and from a place which specialized in
recorded sound effects he ordered several records of clapping and
25 applauding by enthusiastic audiences. Finally he bought himself a
conductor's baton, a slim ivory stick which lay in a case lined with
blue silk.

In eight days the room was ready. Everything was perfect; the
red chairs, the aisle down the centre and even a little dais on the
30 platform with a brass rail running round it for the conductor.
Mr Botibol decided to give the first concert that evening after
dinner.

At seven o'clock he went up to his bedroom and changed into
white tie and tails. He felt marvellous. When he looked at himself
35 in the mirror, the sight of his own grotesque shoulderless figure
didn't worry him in the least. A great composer, he thought, smiling,

can look as he damn well pleases. People *expect* him to look peculiar. All the same he wished he had some hair on his head. He would have liked to let it grow rather long. He went downstairs to dinner, ate his food rapidly, drank half a bottle of wine and felt better still. 'Don't worry about me, Mason,' he said. 'I'm not mad. I'm just enjoying myself.'

'Yes, sir.'

'I shan't want you any more. Please see that I'm not disturbed.' Mr Botibol went from the dining-room into the miniature concert-hall. He took out the records of Beethoven's First Symphony, but before putting them on the gramophone, he placed two other records with them. The one, which was to be played first of all, before the music began, was labelled 'prolonged enthusiastic applause'. The other, which would come at the end of the symphony, was labelled 'Sustained applause, clapping, cheering, shouts of encore'. By a simple mechanical device on the record changer, the gramophone people had arranged that the sound from the first and the last records – the applause – would come only from the loudspeaker in the auditorium. The sound from all the others – the music – would come from the speaker hidden among the chairs of the orchestra. When he had arranged the records in the concert order, he placed them on the machine but he didn't switch on at once. Instead he turned out all the lights in the room except one small one which lit up the conductor's dais and he sat down in the chair up on the stage, closed his eyes and allowed his thoughts to wander into the usual delicious regions; the great composer, nervous, impatient, waiting to present his latest masterpiece, the audience assembling, the murmur of their excited talk, and so on. Having dreamed himself right into the part, he stood up, picked up his baton and switched on the gramophone.

A tremendous wave of clapping filled the room. Mr Botibol walked across the stage, mounted the dais, faced the audience and bowed. In the darkness he could just make out the faint outline of the seats on either side of the centre aisle, but he couldn't see the faces of the people. They were making enough noise. What an ovation! Mr Botibol turned and faced the orchestra. The applause behind him died down. The next record dropped. The symphony began.

This time it was more thrilling than ever, and during the performance he registered any number of prickly sensations around his
5 solar plexus. Once, when it suddenly occurred to him that the
music was being broadcast all over the world, a sort of shiver ran
right down the length of his spine. But by far the most exciting
part was the applause which came at the end. They cheered and
clapped and stamped and shouted encore! encore! encore! and
10 he turned towards the darkened auditorium and bowed gravely to
the left and right. Then he went off the stage, but they called
him back. He bowed several more times and went off again, and
again they called him back. The audience had gone mad. They
simply wouldn't let him go. It was terrific. It was truly a terrific
15 ovation.

Later, when he was resting in his chair in the other room, he
was still enjoying it. He closed his eyes because he didn't want
anything to break the spell. He lay there and he felt like he was
floating. It was really a most marvellous floating feeling, and when
20 he went upstairs and undressed and got into bed, it was still with
him.

The following evening he conducted Beethoven's – or rather
Botibol's – Second Symphony, and they were just as mad about
that one as the first. The next few nights he played one symphony
25 a night, and at the end of nine evenings he had worked through all
nine of Beethoven's symphonies. It got more exciting every time
because before each concert the audience kept saying, 'He can't
do it again, not another masterpiece. It's not humanly possible.'
But he did. They were all of them equally magnificent. The last
30 symphony, the Ninth, was especially exciting because here the
composer surprised and delighted everyone by suddenly providing
a choral masterpiece. He had to conduct a huge choir as well as
the orchestra itself, and Benjamino Gigli had flown over from Italy
to take the tenor part. Enrico Pinza sang bass. At the end of it the
35 audience shouted themselves hoarse. The whole musical world
was on its feet cheering, and on all sides they were saying how you

never could tell what wonderful things to expect next from this amazing person.

The composing, presenting and conducting of nine great symphonies in as many days is a fair achievement for any man, and it was not astonishing that it went a little to Mr Botibol's head. He decided now that he would once again surprise his public. He would compose a mass of marvellous piano music and he himself would give the recitals. So early the next morning he set out for the show room of the people who sold Bechsteins and Steinways. He felt so brisk and fit that he walked all the way, and as he walked he hummed little snatches of new and lovely tunes for the piano. His head was full of them. All the time they kept coming to him and once, suddenly, he had the feeling the thousands of small notes, some white, some black, were cascading down a chute into his head through a hole in his head, and that his brain, his amazing musical brain, was receiving them as fast as they could come and unscrambling them and arranging them neatly in a certain order so that they made wondrous melodies. There were Nocturnes, there were Études and there were Waltzes, and soon, he told himself, soon he would give them all to a grateful and admiring world.

When he arrived at the piano-shop, he pushed the door open and walked in with an air almost of confidence. He had changed much in the last few days. Some of his nervousness had left him and he was no longer wholly preoccupied with what others thought of his appearance. 'I want,' he said to the salesman, 'a concert grand, but you must arrange it so that when the notes are struck, no sound is produced.'

The salesman leaned forward and raised his eyebrows.

'Could that be arranged?' Mr Botibol asked.

'Yes, sir, I think so, if you desire it. But might I inquire what you intend to use the instrument for?'

'If you want to know, I'm going to pretend I'm Chopin. I'm going to sit and play while a gramophone makes the music. It gives me a kick.' It came out, just like that, and Mr Botibol didn't know what had made him say it. But it was done now and he had said it and that was that. In a way he felt relieved, because he had proved he didn't mind telling people what he was doing. The man would probably answer what a jolly good idea. Or he might not. He might say well you ought to be locked up.

5 'So now you know,' Mr Botibol said.

The salesman laughed out loud. 'Ha ha! Ha ha ha! That's very good, sir. Very good indeed. Serves me right for asking silly questions.' He stopped suddenly in the middle of the laugh and looked hard at Mr Botibol. 'Of course, sir, you probably know that
10 we sell a simple noiseless keyboard specially for silent practising.'

'I want a concert grand,' Mr Botibol said. The salesman looked at him again.

Mr Botibol chose his piano and got out of the shop as quickly as possible. He went on to the store that sold gramophone records
15 and there he ordered a quantity of albums containing recordings of all Chopin's Nocturnes, Études and Waltzes, played by Arthur Rubinstein.

'My goodness, you *are* going to have a lovely time!'

Mr Botibol turned and saw standing beside him at the counter
20 a squat, short-legged girl with a face as plain as a pudding.

'Yes,' he answered. 'Oh yes, I am.' Normally he was strict about not speaking to females in public places, but this one had taken him by surprise.

'I love Chopin,' the girl said. She was holding a slim brown paper
25 bag with string handles containing a single record she had just bought. 'I like him better than any of the others.'

It was comforting to hear the voice of this girl after the way the piano salesman had laughed. Mr Botibol wanted to talk to her but he didn't know what to say.

30 The girl said, 'I like the Nocturnes best, they're so soothing. Which are your favourites?'

Mr Botibol said, 'Well . . .' The girl looked up at him and she smiled pleasantly, trying to assist with his embarrassment. It was the smile that did it. He suddenly found himself saying, 'Well now,
35 perhaps, would you, I wonder . . . I mean I was wondering . . .'

She smiled again; she couldn't help it this time. 'What I mean is I would be glad if you would care to come along some time and listen to these records.'

'Why how nice of you.' She paused, wondering whether it was all right. 'You really mean it?'

'Yes, I should be glad.'                                                        5

She had lived long enough in the city to discover that old men, if they are dirty old men, do not bother about trying to pick up a girl as unattractive as herself. Only twice in her life had she been accosted in public and each time the man had been drunk. But this one wasn't drunk. He was nervous and he was peculiar-looking,   10
but he wasn't drunk. Come to think of it, it was she who had started the conversation in the first place. 'It would be lovely,' she said. 'It really would. When could I come?'

Oh dear, Mr Botibol thought. Oh dear, oh dear, oh dear, oh dear.                                                                            15

'I could come tomorrow,' she went on. 'It's my afternoon off.'

'Well, yes, certainly,' he answered slowly. 'Yes, of course. I'll give you my card. Here it is.'

'A. W. Botibol,' she read aloud. 'What a funny name. Mine's Darlington. Miss L. Darlington. How d'you do, Mr Botibol.' She   20
put out her hand for him to shake. 'Oh I *am* looking forward to this! What time shall I come?'

'Any time,' he said. 'Please come any time.'

'Three o'clock?'

'Yes. Three o'clock.'                                                           25

'Lovely! I'll be there.'

He watched her walk out of the shop, a squat, stumpy, thick-legged little person and my word, he thought, what have I done! He was amazed at himself. But he was not displeased. Then at once he started to worry about whether or not he should let her   30
see his concert-hall. He worried still more when he realized that it was the only place in the house where there was a gramophone.

That evening he had no concert. Instead he sat in his chair brooding about Miss Darlington and what he should do when she arrived. The next morning they brought the piano, a fine Bechstein   35
in dark mahogany which was carried in minus its legs and later

assembled on the platform in the concert hall. It was an imposing instrument and when Mr Botibol opened it and pressed a note with his finger, it made no sound at all. He had originally intended to astonish the world with a recital of his first piano compositions
5 – a set of Études – as soon as the piano arrived, but it was no good now. He was too worried about Miss Darlington and three o'clock. At lunch-time his trepidation had increased and he couldn't eat. 'Mason,' he said, 'I'm, I'm expecting a young lady to call at three o'clock.'

10     'A what, sir?' the butler said.
       'A young lady, Mason.'
       'Very good, sir.'
       'Show her into the sitting-room.'
       'Yes, sir.'

15     Precisely at three he heard the bell ring. A few moments later Mason was showing her into the room. She came in, smiling, and Mr Botibol stood up and shook her hand. 'My!' she exclaimed. 'What a lovely house! I didn't know I was calling on a millionaire!'

20     She settled her small plump body into a large armchair and Mr Botibol sat opposite. He didn't know what to say. He felt terrible. But almost at once she began to talk and she chattered away gaily about this and that for a long time without stopping. Mostly it was about his house and the furniture and the carpets and about how
25 nice it was of him to invite her because she didn't have such an awful lot of excitement in her life. She worked hard all day and she shared a room with two other girls in a boarding-house and he could have no idea how thrilling it was for her to be here. Gradually Mr Botibol began to feel better. He sat there listening to the girl,
30 rather liking her, nodding his bald head slowly up and down, and the more she talked, the more he liked her. She was gay and chatty, but underneath all that any fool could see that she was a lonely tired little thing. Even Mr Botibol could see that. He could see it very clearly indeed. It was at this point that he began to play with
35 a daring and risky idea.

       'Miss Darlington,' he said. 'I'd like to show you something.' He led her out of the room straight to the little concert-hall. 'Look,' he said.

She stopped just inside the door. 'My goodness! Just look at that! A theatre! A real little theatre!' Then she saw the piano on the platform and the conductor's dais with the brass rail running round it. 'It's for concerts!' she cried. 'Do you really have concerts here! Oh, Mr Botibol, how exciting!'

'Do you like it?'

'Oh yes!'

'Come back into the other room and I'll tell you about it.' Her enthusiasm had given him confidence and he wanted to get going. 'Come back and listen while I tell you something funny.' And when they were seated in the sitting-room again, he began at once to tell her his story. He told the whole thing, right from the beginning, how one day, listening to a symphony, he had imagined himself to be the composer, how he had stood up and started to conduct, how he had got an immense pleasure out of it, how he had done it again with similar results and how finally he had built himself the concert-hall where already he had conducted nine symphonies. But he cheated a little bit in the telling. He said that the only real reason he did it was in order to obtain the maximum appreciation from the music. There was only one way to listen to music, he told her, only one way to make yourself listen to every single note and chord. You had to do two things at once. You had to imagine that you had composed it, and at the same time you had to imagine that the public were hearing it for the first time. 'Do you think,' he said, 'do you really think that any outsider has ever got half as great a thrill from a symphony as the composer himself when he first heard his work played by a full orchestra?'

'No,' she answered timidly. 'Of course not.'

'Then become the composer! Steal his music! Take it away from him and give it to yourself!' He leaned back in his chair and for the first time she saw him smile. He had only just thought of this new complex explanation of his conduct, but to him it seemed a very good one and he smiled. 'Well, what do you think, Miss Darlington?'

'I must say it's very very interesting.' She was polite and puzzled but she was a long way away from him now.

'Would you like to try?'

'Oh no. Please.'

5 'I wish you would.'

'I'm afraid I don't think I should be able to feel the same way as you do about it, Mr Botibol. I don't think I have a strong enough imagination.'

She could see from his eyes he was disappointed. 'But I'd love
10 to sit in the audience and listen while you do it,' she added.

Then he leapt up from his chair. 'I've got it!' he cried. 'A piano concerto! You play the piano, I conduct. You the greatest pianist, the greatest in the world. First performance of my Piano Concerto No. 1. You playing, me conducting. The greatest pianist and
15 the greatest composer together for the first time. A tremendous occasion! The audience will go mad! There'll be queueing all night outside the hall to get in. It'll be broadcast around the world. It'll, it'll . . .' Mr Botibol stopped. He stood behind the chair with both hands resting on the back of the chair and suddenly he looked
20 embarrassed and a trifle sheepish. 'I'm sorry,' he said, 'I get worked up. You see how it is. Even the thought of another performance gets me worked up.' And then plaintively, 'Would you, Miss Darlington, would you play a piano concerto with me?'

'It's like children,' she said, but she smiled.

25 'No one will know. No one but us will know anything about it.'

'All right,' she said at last. 'I'll do it. I think I'm daft but just the same I'll do it. It'll be a bit of a lark.'

'Good!' Mr Botibol cried. 'When? Tonight?'

30 'Oh well, I don't . . .'

'Yes,' he said eagerly. 'Please. Make it tonight. Come back and have dinner here with me and we'll give the concert afterwards.' Mr Botibol was excited again now. 'We must make a few plans. Which is your favourite piano concerto, Miss Darlington?'

35 'Oh well, I should say Beethoven's Emperor.'

'The Emperor it shall be. You will play it tonight. Come to

dinner at seven. Evening dress. You must have evening dress for the concert.'

'I've got a dancing dress but I haven't worn it for years.'

'You shall wear it tonight.' He paused and looked at her in silence for a moment, then quite gently, he said, 'You're not worried, Miss Darlington? Perhaps you would rather not do it. I'm afraid, I'm afraid I've let myself get rather carried away. I seem to have pushed you into this. And I know how stupid it must seem to you.'

That's better, she thought. That's much better. Now I know it's all right. 'Oh no,' she said. 'I'm really looking forward to it. But you frightened me a bit, taking it all so seriously.'

When she had gone, he waited for five minutes, then went out into the town to the gramophone shop and bought the records of the Emperor Concerto, conductor, Toscanini – soloist, Horowitz. He turned at once, told his astonished butler that there would be a guest for dinner, then went upstairs and changed into his tails.

She arrived at seven. She was wearing a long sleeveless dress made of some shiny green material and to Mr Botibol she did not look quite so plump or quite so plain as before. He took her straight in to dinner and in spite of the silent disapproving manner in which Mason prowled around the table, the meal went well. She protested gaily when Mr Botibol gave her a second glass of wine, but she didn't refuse it. She chattered away almost without a stop throughout the three courses and Mr Botibol listened and nodded and kept refilling her glass as soon as it was half empty.

Afterwards, when they were seated in the living-room, Mr Botibol said, 'Now Miss Darlington, now we begin to fall into our parts.' The wine, as usual, had made him happy, and the girl, who was even less used to it than the man, was not feeling so bad either. 'You, Miss Darlington, are the great pianist. What is your first name, Miss Darlington?'

'Lucille,' she said.

'The great pianist Lucille Darlington. I am the composer Botibol. We must talk and act and think as though we are pianist and composer.'

'What is *your* first name, Mr Botibol? What does the A stand for?'

'Angel,' he answered.

'Not Angel.'

5 'Yes,' he said irritably.

'Angel Botibol,' she murmured and she began to giggle. But she checked herself and said, 'I think it's a most unusual and distinguished name.'

'Are you ready, Miss Darlington?'

10 'Yes.'

Mr Botibol stood up and began pacing nervously up and down the room. He looked at his watch. 'It's nearly time to go on,' he said. 'They tell me the place is packed. Not an empty seat anywhere. I always get nervous before a concert. Do you get nervous, Miss 15 Darlington?'

'Oh yes, I do, always. Especially playing with you.'

'I think they'll like it. I put everything I've got into this concerto, Miss Darlington. It nearly killed me composing it. I was ill for weeks afterwards.'

20 'Poor you,' she said.

'It's time now,' he said. 'The orchestra are all in their places. Come on.' He led her out and down the passage, then he made her wait outside the door of the concert-hall while he nipped in, arranged the lighting and switched on the gramophone. He came 25 back and fetched her and as they walked on to the stage, the applause broke out. They both stood and bowed towards the darkened auditorium and the applause was vigorous and it went on for a long time. Then Mr Botibol mounted the dais and Miss Darlington took her seat at the piano. The applause died down. 30 Mr Botibol held up his baton. The next record dropped and the Emperor Concerto began.

It was an astonishing affair. The thin stalk-like Mr Botibol, who had no shoulders, standing on the dais in his evening clothes waving his arms about in approximate time to the music; and the plump 35 Miss Darlington in her shiny green dress seated at the keyboard of the enormous piano thumping the silent keys with both hands for all she was worth. She recognized the passages where the piano was meant to be silent, and on these occasions she folded her hands primly on her lap and stared straight ahead with a dreamy and enraptured expression on her face. Watching her, Mr Botibol thought that she was particularly wonderful in the slow solo passages of the Second Movement. She allowed her hands to drift smoothly and gently up and down the keys and she inclined her head first to one side, then to the other, and once she closed her eyes for a long time while she played. During the exciting last movement, Mr Botibol himself lost his balance and would have fallen off the platform had he not saved himself by clutching the brass rail. But in spite of everything, the concerto moved on majestically to its mighty conclusion. Then the real clapping came. Mr Botibol walked over and took Miss Darlington by the hand and led her to the edge of the platform, and there they stood, the two of them, bowing, and bowing, and bowing again as the clapping and the shouting of 'encore' continued. Four times they left the stage and came back, and then, the fifth time, Mr Botibol whispered, 'It's you they want. You take this one alone.' 'No,' she said. 'It's you. Please.' But he pushed her forward and she took her call, and came back and said, 'Now you. They want you. Can't you hear them shouting for you?' So Mr Botibol walked alone on to the stage, bowed gravely to right, left and centre and came off just as the clapping stopped altogether.

He led her straight back to the living-room. He was breathing fast and the sweat was pouring down all over his face. She too was a little breathless, and her cheeks were shining red.

'A tremendous performance, Miss Darlington. Allow me to congratulate you.'

'But what a concerto, Mr Botibol! What a superb concerto!'

'You played it perfectly, Miss Darlington. You have a real feeling for my music.' He was wiping the sweat from his face with a handkerchief. 'And tomorrow we perform my Second Concerto.'

'Tomorrow?'

'Of course. Had you forgotten, Miss Darlington? We are booked to appear together for a whole week.'

'Oh . . . oh yes . . . I'm afraid I had forgotten that.'

'But it's all right, isn't it?' he asked anxiously. 'After hearing you tonight I could not bear to have anyone else play my music.'

'I think it's all right,' she said. 'Yes, I think that'll be all right.' She looked at the clock on the mantelpiece. 'My heavens, it's late!
5  I must go! I'll never get up in the morning to get to work!'

'To work?' Mr Botibol said. 'To work?' Then slowly, reluctantly, he forced himself back to reality. 'Ah yes, to work. Of course, you have to get to work.'

'I certainly do.'

10  'Where do you work, Miss Darlington?'

'Me? Well,' and now she hesitated a moment, looking at Mr Botibol. 'As a matter of fact I work at the old Academy.'

'I hope it is pleasant work,' he said. 'What Academy is that?'

'I teach the piano.'

15  Mr Botibol jumped as though someone had stuck him from behind with a hatpin. His mouth opened very wide.

'It's quite all right,' she said, smiling. 'I've always wanted to be Horowitz. And could I, do you think, could I please be Schnabel tomorrow?'

# My Lady Love, My Dove

It has been my habit for many years to take a nap after lunch. I settle myself in a chair in the living-room with a cushion behind my head and my feet up on a small square leather stool, and I read until I drop off.

On this Friday afternoon, I was in my chair and feeling as comfortable as ever with a book in my hands – an old favourite, Doubleday and Westwood's *The Genera of Diurnal Lepidoptera* – when my wife, who has never been a silent lady, began to talk to me from the sofa opposite. 'These two people,' she said, 'what time are they coming?'

I made no answer, so she repeated the question, louder this time.

I told her politely that I didn't know.

'I don't think I like them very much,' she said. 'Especially him.'

'No dear, all right.'

'Arthur. I said I don't think I like them very much.'

I lowered my book and looked across at her lying with her feet up on the sofa, flipping over the pages of some fashion magazine. 'We've only met them once,' I said.

'A dreadful man, really. Never stopped telling jokes, or stories, or something.'

'I'm sure you'll manage them very well, dear.'

'And she's pretty frightful, too. When do you think they'll arrive?'

Somewhere around six o'clock, I guessed.

'But don't *you* think they're awful?' she asked, pointing at me with her finger.

'Well . . .'

'They're *too* awful, they really are.'

'We can hardly put them off now, Pamela.'

'They're absolutely the end,' she said.

'Then why did you ask them?' The question slipped out before I could stop myself and I regretted it at once, for it is a rule with 5 me never to provoke my wife if I can help it. There was a pause, and I watched her face, waiting for the answer – the big white face that to me was something so strange and fascinating there were occasions when I could hardly bring myself to look away from it. In the evenings sometimes – working on her embroidery, or painting 10 those small intricate flower pictures – the face would tighten and glimmer with a subtle inward strength that was beautiful beyond words, and I would sit and stare at it minute after minute while pretending to read. Even now, at this moment, with that compressed acid look, the frowning forehead, the petulant curl of the 15 nose, I had to admit that there was a majestic quality about this woman, something splendid, almost stately; and so tall she was, far taller than I – although today, in her fifty-first year, I think one would have to call her big rather than tall.

'You know very well why I asked them,' she answered sharply. 20 'For bridge, that's all. They play an absolutely first-class game, and for a decent stake.' She glanced up and saw me watching her. 'Well,' she said, 'that's about the way you feel too, isn't it?'

'Well, of course, I . . .'

'Don't be a fool, Arthur.'

25 'The only time I met them I must say they did seem quite nice.'

'So is the butcher.'

'Now Pamela, dear – please. We don't want any of that.'

'Listen,' she said, slapping down the magazine on her lap, 'you saw the sort of people they were as well as I did. A pair of stupid 30 climbers who think they can go anywhere just because they play good bridge.'

'I'm sure you're right dear, but what I don't honestly understand is why –'

'I keep telling you – so that for once we can get a decent game. 35 I'm sick and tired of playing with rabbits. But I really can't see why I should have these awful people in the house.'

'Of course not, my dear, but isn't it a little late now –'

'Arthur?'

'Yes?'

'Why for God's sake do you always argue with me? You *know* you disliked them as much as I did.'

'I really don't think you need worry, Pamela. After all, they seemed quite a nice well-mannered young couple.'

'Arthur, don't be pompous.' She was looking at me hard with those wide grey eyes of hers, and to avoid them – they sometimes made me quite uncomfortable – I got up and walked over to the french windows that led into the garden.

The big sloping lawn out in front of the house was newly mown, striped with pale and dark ribbons of green. On the far side, the two laburnums were in full flower at last, the long golden chains making a blaze of colour against the darker trees beyond. The roses were out too, and the scarlet begonias, and in the long herbaceous border all my lovely hybrid lupins, columbine, delphinium, sweet-william, and the huge pale, scented iris. One of the gardeners was coming up the drive from his lunch. I could see the roof of his cottage through the trees, and beyond it to one side, the place where the drive went out through the iron gates on the Canterbury road.

My wife's house. Her garden. How beautiful it all was! How peaceful! Now, if only Pamela would try to be a little less solicitous of my welfare, less prone to coax me into doing things for my own good rather than for my own pleasure, then everything would be heaven. Mind you, I don't want to give the impression that I do not love her – I worship the very air she breathes – or that I can't manage her, or that I am not the captain of my ship. All I am trying to say is that she can be a trifle irritating at times, the way she carries on. For example, those little mannerisms of hers – I do wish she would drop them all, especially the way she has of pointing a finger at me to emphasize a phrase. You must remember that I am a man who is built rather small, and a gesture like this, when used to excess by a person like my wife, is apt to intimidate. I sometimes find it difficult to convince myself that she is not an overbearing woman.

'Arthur!' she called. 'Come here.'

'What?'

'I've just had a most marvellous idea. Come here.'

I turned and went over to where she was lying on the sofa.

5   'Look,' she said, 'do you want to have some fun?'

'What sort of fun?'

'With the Snapes?'

'Who are the Snapes?'

'Come on,' she said. 'Wake up. Henry and Sally Snape. Our
10 weekend guests.'

'Well?'

'Now listen. I was lying here thinking how awful they really are . . .
the way they behave . . . him with his jokes and her like a sort of
love-crazed sparrow . . .' She hesitated, smiling slyly, and for some
15 reason, I got the impression she was about to say a shocking thing.
'Well – if that's the way they behave when they're in front of us, then
what on earth must they be like when they're alone together?'

'Now wait a minute, Pamela –'

'Don't be an ass, Arthur. Let's have some fun – some real fun
20 for once – tonight.' She had half raised herself up off the sofa, her
face bright with a kind of sudden recklessness, the mouth slightly
open, and she was looking at me with two round grey eyes, a spark
dancing slowly in each.

'Why shouldn't we?'

25   'What do you want to do?'

'Why, it's obvious. Can't you see?'

'No, I can't.'

'All we've got to do is put a microphone in their room.' I admit
I was expecting something pretty bad, but when she said this I was
30 so shocked I didn't know what to answer.

'That's exactly what we'll do,' she said.

'Here!' I cried. 'No. Wait a minute. You can't do that.'

'Why not?'

'That's about the nastiest trick I ever heard of. It's like – why,
35 it's like listening at keyholes, or reading letters, only far far worse.
You don't mean this seriously, do you?'

'Of course I do.'

I knew how much she disliked being contradicted, but there were times when I felt it necessary to assert myself, even at considerable risk. 'Pamela,' I said, snapping the words out, 'I forbid you to do it!'

She took her feet down from the sofa and sat up straight. 'What in God's name are you trying to pretend to be, Arthur? I simply don't understand you.'

'That shouldn't be too difficult.'

'Tommyrot! I've known you do lots of worse things than this before now.'

'Never!'

'Oh yes I have. What makes you suddenly think you're a so much nicer person than I am?'

'I've never done things like that.'

'All right, my boy,' she said, pointing her finger at me like a pistol. 'What about that time at the Milfords' last Christmas? Remember? You nearly laughed your head off and I had to put my hand over your mouth to stop them hearing us. What about that for one?'

'That was different,' I said. 'It wasn't our house. And they weren't our guests.'

'It doesn't make any difference at all.' She was sitting very upright, staring at me with those round grey eyes, and the chin was beginning to come up high in a peculiarly contemptuous manner. 'Don't be such a pompous hypocrite,' she said. 'What on earth's come over you?'

'I really think it's a pretty nasty thing, you know, Pamela. I honestly do.'

'But listen, Arthur. I'm a *nasty* person. And so are you – in a secret sort of way. That's why we get along together.'

'I never heard such nonsense.'

'Mind you, if you've suddenly decided to change your character completely, that's another story.'

'You've got to stop talking this way, Pamela.'

'You see,' she said, 'if you really *have* decided to reform, then what on earth am I going to do?'

'You don't know what you're saying.'

'Arthur, how could a nice person like you want to associate with a stinker?'

I sat myself down slowly in the chair opposite her, and she was watching me all the time. You understand, she was a big woman, with a big white face, and when she looked at me hard, as she was doing now, I became – how shall I say it – surrounded, almost enveloped by her, as though she were a great tub of cream and I had fallen in.

'You don't honestly want to do this microphone thing, do you?'

'But of course I do. It's time we had a bit of fun around here. Come on, Arthur. Don't be so stuffy.'

'It's not right, Pamela.'

'It's just as right' – up came the finger again – 'just as right as when you found those letters of Mary Probert's in her purse and you read them through from beginning to end.'

'We should never have done that.'

'*We!*'

'You read them afterwards, Pamela.'

'It didn't harm anyone at all. You said so yourself at the time. And this one's no worse.'

'How would *you* like it if someone did it to *you*?'

'How could I *mind* if I didn't know it was being done? Come on, Arthur. Don't be so flabby.'

'I'll have to think about it.'

'Maybe the great radio engineer doesn't know how to connect the mike to the speaker?'

'That's the easiest part.'

'Well, go on then. Go on and do it.'

'I'll think about it and let you know later.'

'There's no time for that. They might arrive any moment.'

'Then I won't do it. I'm not going to be caught red-handed.'

'If they come before you're through, I'll simply keep them down here. No danger. What's the time, anyway?'

It was nearly three o'clock.

'They're driving down from London,' she said, 'and they certainly won't leave till after lunch. That gives you plenty of time.'

'Which room are you putting them in?'

'The big yellow room at the end of the corridor. That's not too far away, is it?'

'I suppose it could be done.'

'And by the by,' she said, 'where are you going to have the speaker?'

'I haven't said I'm going to do it yet.'

'My God!' she cried, 'I'd like to see someone try and stop you now. You ought to see your face. It's all pink and excited at the very prospect. Put the speaker in our bedroom why not? But go on – and hurry.'

I hesitated. It was something I made a point of doing whenever she tried to order me about, instead of asking nicely. 'I don't like it, Pamela.'

She didn't say any more after that; she just sat there, absolutely still, watching me, a resigned, waiting expression on her face, as though she were in a long queue. This, I knew from experience, was a danger signal. She was like one of those bomb things with the pin pulled out, and it was only a matter of time before – bang! and she would explode. In the silence that followed, I could almost hear her ticking.

So I got up quietly and went out to the workshop and collected a mike and a hundred and fifty feet of wire. Now that I was away from her, I am ashamed to admit that I began to feel a bit of excitement myself, a tiny warm prickling sensation under the skin, near the tips of my fingers. It was nothing much, mind you – really nothing at all. Good heavens, I experience the same thing every morning of my life when I open the paper to check the closing prices on two or three of my wife's larger stockholdings. So I wasn't going to get carried away by a silly joke like this. At the same time, I couldn't help being amused.

I took the stairs two at a time and entered the yellow room at the end of the passage. It had the clean, unlived-in appearance of all guest rooms, with its twin beds, yellow satin bedspreads,

pale-yellow walls, and golden-coloured curtains. I began to look around for a good place to hide the mike. This was the most important part of all, for whatever happened, it must not be discovered. I thought first of the basket of logs by the fireplace. Put
5  it under the logs. No – not safe enough. Behind the radiator? On top of the wardrobe? Under the desk? None of these seemed very professional to me. All might be subject to chance inspection because of a dropped collar stud or something like that. Finally, with considerable cunning, I decided to put it inside the springing
10  of the sofa. The sofa was against the wall, near the edge of the carpet, and my lead wire could go straight under the carpet over to the door.

    I tipped up the sofa and slit the material underneath. Then I tied the microphone securely up among the springs, making sure
15  that it faced the room. After that, I led the wire under the carpet to the door. I was calm and cautious in everything I did. Where the wire had to emerge from under the carpet and pass out of the door, I made a little groove in the wood so that it was almost invisible.

20    All this, of course, took time, and when I suddenly heard the crunch of wheels on the gravel of the drive outside, and then the slamming of car doors and the voices of our guests, I was still only half-way down the corridor, tacking the wire along the skirting. I stopped and straightened up, hammer in hand, and I must confess
25  that I felt afraid. You have no idea how unnerving that noise was to me. I experienced the same sudden stomachy feeling of fright as when a bomb once dropped the other side of the village during the war, one afternoon, while I was working quietly in the library with my butterflies.

30    Don't worry, I told myself. Pamela will take care of these people. She won't let them come up here.

    Rather frantically, I set about finishing the job, and soon I had the wire tacked all along the corridor and through into our bedroom. Here, concealment was not so important, although I still did not
35  permit myself to get careless because of the servants. So I laid the wire under the carpet and brought it up unobtrusively into the

back of the radio. Making the final connections was an elementary technical matter and took me no time at all.

Well – I had done it. I stepped back and glanced at the little radio. Somehow, now, it looked different – no longer a silly box for making noises but an evil little creature that crouched on the table top with a part of its own body reaching out secretly into a forbidden place far away. I switched it on. It hummed faintly but made no other sound. I took my bedside clock, which had a loud tick, and carried it along to the yellow room and placed it on the floor by the sofa. When I returned, sure enough the radio creature was ticking away as loudly as if the clock were in the room – even louder.

I fetched back the clock. Then I tidied myself up in the bathroom, returned my tools to the workshop, and prepared to meet the guests. But first, to compose myself, and so that I would not have to appear in front of them with the blood, as it were, still wet on my hands, I spent five minutes in the library with my collection. I concentrated on a tray of the lovely *Vanessa cardui* – the 'painted lady' – and made a few notes for a paper I was preparing entitled 'The Relation between Colour Pattern and Framework of Wings', which I intended to read at the next meeting of our society in Canterbury. In this way I soon regained my normal grave, attentive manner.

When I entered the living-room, our two guests, whose names I could never remember, were seated on the sofa. My wife was mixing drinks.

'Oh, *there* you are, Arthur,' she said. 'Where *have* you been?'

I thought this was an unnecessary remark. 'I'm so sorry,' I said to the guests as we shook hands. 'I was busy and forgot the time.'

'We all know what *you've* been doing,' the girl said, smiling wisely. 'But we'll forgive him, won't we, dearest?'

'I think we should,' the husband answered.

I had a frightful, fantastic vision of my wife telling them, amidst roars of laughter, precisely what I had been doing upstairs. She *couldn't* – she *couldn't* have done that! I looked round at her and she too was smiling as she measured out the gin.

'I'm sorry we disturbed you,' the girl said.

I decided that if this was going to be a joke then I'd better join in quickly, so I forced myself to smile with her.

'You must let us see it,' the girl continued.

5 'See what?'

'Your collection. Your wife says that they are absolutely beautiful.'

I lowered myself slowly into a chair and relaxed. It was ridiculous to be so nervous and jumpy. 'Are you interested in butterflies?' I
10 asked her.

'I'd love to see yours, Mr Beauchamp.'

The martinis were distributed and we settled down to a couple of hours of talk and drink before dinner. It was from then on that I began to form the impression that our guests were a charming
15 couple. My wife, coming from a titled family, is apt to be conscious of her class and breeding, and is often hasty in her judgement of strangers who are friendly towards her – particularly tall men. She is frequently right, but in this case I felt that she might be making a mistake. As a rule, I myself do not like tall men either; they are
20 apt to be supercilious and omniscient. But Henry Snape – my wife had whispered his name – struck me as being an amiable simple young man with good manners whose main preoccupation, very properly, was Mrs Snape. He was handsome in a long-faced, horsy sort of way, with dark-brown eyes that seemed to be gentle and
25 sympathetic. I envied him his fine mop of black hair, and caught myself wondering what lotion he used to keep it looking so healthy. He did tell us one or two jokes, but they were on a high level and no one could have objected.

'At school,' he said, 'they used to call me Scervix. Do you know
30 why?'

'I haven't the least idea,' my wife answered.

'Because cervix is Latin for nape.'

This was rather deep and it took me a while to work out.

'What school was that, Mr Snape?' my wife asked.

35 'Eton,' he said, and my wife gave a quick little nod of approval. Now she will talk to him, I thought, so I turned my attention to

the other one, Sally Snape. She was an attractive girl with a bosom. Had I met her fifteen years earlier I might well have got myself into some sort of trouble. As it was, I had a pleasant enough time telling her all about my beautiful butterflies. I was observing her closely as I talked, and after a while I began to get the impression that she was not, in fact, quite so merry and smiling a girl as I had been led to believe at first. She seemed to be coiled in herself, as though with a secret she was jealously guarding. The deep-blue eyes moved too quickly about the room, never settling or resting on one thing for more than a moment; and over all her face, though so faint that they might not even have been there, those small downward lines of sorrow.

'I'm so looking forward to our game of bridge,' I said, finally changing the subject.

'Us too,' she answered. 'You know we play almost every night, we love it so.'

'You are extremely expert, both of you. How did you get to be so good?'

'It's practice,' she said. 'That's all. Practice, practice, practice.'

'Have you played in any championships?'

'Not yet, but Henry wants very much for us to do that. It's hard work, you know, to reach that standard. Terribly hard work.' Was there not here, I wondered, a hint of resignation in her voice? Yes, that was probably it; he was pushing her too hard, making her take it too seriously, and the poor girl was tired of it all.

At eight o'clock, without changing, we moved in to dinner. The meal went well, with Henry Snape telling us some very droll stories. He also praised my Richebourg '34 in a most knowledgeable fashion, which pleased me greatly. By the time coffee came, I realized that I had grown to like these two youngsters immensely, and as a result I began to feel uncomfortable about this microphone business. It would have been all right if they had been horrid people, but to play this trick on two such charming young persons as these filled me with a strong sense of guilt. Don't misunderstand me. I was not getting cold feet. It didn't seem necessary to stop the operation. But I refused to relish the prospect openly as my wife seemed now to be doing, with covert smiles and winks and secret little noddings of the head.

Around nine-thirty, feeling comfortable and well fed, we returned to the large living-room to start our bridge. We were playing for a fair stake – ten shillings a hundred – so we decided not to split families, and I partnered my wife the whole time. We all four of us took the game seriously, which is the only way to take it, and we played silently, intently, hardly speaking at all except to bid. It was not the money we played for. Heaven knows, my wife had enough of that, and so apparently did the Snapes. But among experts it is almost traditional that they play for a reasonable stake.

That night the cards were evenly divided, but for once my wife played badly, so we got the worst of it. I could see that she wasn't concentrating fully, and as we came along towards midnight she began not even to care. She kept glancing up at me with those large grey eyes of hers, the eyebrows raised, the nostrils curiously open, a little gloating smile around the corner of her mouth.

Our opponents played a fine game. Their bidding was masterly, and all through the evening they made only one mistake. That was when the girl badly overestimated her partner's hand and bid six spades. I doubled and they went three down, vulnerable, which cost them eight hundred points. It was just a momentary lapse, but I remember that Sally Snape was very put out by it, even though her husband forgave her at once, kissing her hand across the table and telling her not to worry.

Around twelve-thirty my wife announced that she wanted to go to bed.

'Just one more rubber?' Henry Snape said.

'No, Mr Snape. I'm tired tonight. Arthur's tired, too. I can see it. Let's all go to bed.'

She herded us out of the room and we went upstairs, the four of us together. On the way up, there was the usual talk about breakfast and what they wanted and how they were to call the maid. 'I think you'll like your room,' my wife said. 'It has a view right across the valley, and the sun comes to you in the morning around ten o'clock.'

We were in the passage now, standing outside our own bedroom door, and I could see the wire I had put down that afternoon and how it ran along the top of the skirting down to their room. Although it was nearly the same colour as the paint, it looked very conspicuous to me. 'Sleep well,' my wife said. 'Sleep well, Mrs Snape. Good night, Mr Snape.' I followed her into our room and shut the door.

'Quick!' she cried. 'Turn it on!' My wife was always like that, frightened that she was going to miss something. She had a reputation, when she went hunting – I never go myself – of always being right up with the hounds whatever the cost to herself or her horse for fear that she might miss a kill. I could see she had no intention of missing this one.

The little radio warmed up just in time to catch the noise of their door opening and closing again.

'There!' my wife said. 'They've gone in.' She was standing in the centre of the room in her blue dress, her hands clasped before her, her head craned forward, intently listening, and the whole of the big white face seemed somehow to have gathered itself together, tight like a wineskin.

Almost at once the voice of Henry Snape came out of the radio, strong and clear. 'You're just a goddam little fool,' he was saying, and this voice was so different from the one I remembered, so harsh and unpleasant, it made me jump. 'The whole bloody evening wasted! Eight hundred points – that's eight pounds between us!'

'I got mixed up,' the girl answered. 'I won't do it again, I promise.'

'What's *this*?' my wife said. 'What's going on?' Her mouth was wide open now, the eyebrows stretched up high, and she came quickly over to the radio and leaned forward, ear to the speaker. I must say I felt rather excited myself.

'I promise, I promise I won't do it again,' the girl was saying.

'We're not taking any chances,' the man answered grimly. 'We're going to have another practice right now.'

'Oh no, please! I couldn't stand it!'

'Look,' the man said, 'all the way out here to take money off this rich bitch and you have to go and mess it up.'

My wife's turn to jump.

73

'The second time this week,' he went on.

'I promise I won't do it again.'

'Sit down. I'll sing them out and you answer.'

'No, Henry, *please*! Not all five hundred of them. It'll take three
5  hours.'

'All right, then. We'll leave out the finger positions. I think you're
sure of those. We'll just do the basic bids showing honour tricks.'

'Oh, Henry, must we? I'm so tired.'

'It's absolutely essential that you get them perfect,' he said. 'We
10  have a game every day next week, you know that. And we've got
to eat.'

'What is this?' my wife whispered. 'What on earth is it?'

'Shhh!' I said. 'Listen!'

'All right,' the man's voice was saying. 'Now we'll start from the
15  beginning. Ready?'

'Oh Henry, *please*!' She sounded very near to tears.

'Come on, Sally. Pull yourself together.'

Then, in a quite different voice, the one we had been used to
hearing in the living-room, Henry Snape said, '*One* club.' I noticed
20  that there was a curious lilting emphasis on the word 'one', the
first part of the word drawn out long.

'Ace queen of clubs,' the girl replied wearily. 'King jack of spades.
No hearts, and ace jack of diamonds.'

'And how many cards to each suit? Watch my finger positions
25  carefully.'

'You said we could miss those.'

'Well – if you're quite sure you know them?'

'Yes, I know them.'

A pause, then 'A *club*.'

30  'King jack of clubs,' the girl recited. 'Ace of spades. Queen jack
of hearts, and ace queen of diamonds.'

Another pause, then 'I'll say *one* club.'

'Ace king of clubs . . .'

'My heavens alive!' I cried. 'It's a bidding code! They show every
35  card in the hand!'

'Arthur, it couldn't be!'

'It's like those men who go into the audience and borrow something from you and there's a girl blindfold on the stage, and from
the way he phrases the question she can tell him exactly what it is
– even a railway ticket, and what station it's from.'

'It's impossible!'

'Not at all. But it's tremendous hard work to learn. Listen to
them.'

'I'll go *one heart*,' the man's voice was saying.

'King queen ten of hearts. Ace jack of spades. No diamonds.
Queen jack of clubs . . .'

'And you see,' I said, 'he tells her the *number* of cards he has in
each suit by the position of his fingers.'

'How?'

'I don't know. You heard him saying about it.'

'My *God*, Arthur! Are you sure that's what they're doing?'

'I'm afraid so.' I watched her as she walked quickly over to the
side of the bed to fetch a cigarette. She lit it with her back to me
and then swung round, blowing the smoke up at the ceiling in a
thin stream. I knew we were going to have to do something about
this, but I wasn't quite sure what because we couldn't possibly
accuse them without revealing the source of our information. I
waited for my wife's decision.

'Why, Arthur,' she said slowly, blowing out clouds of smoke.
'Why, this is a *mar-vellous* idea. D'you think *we* could learn to do
it?'

'What!'

'Of course. Why not?'

'Here! No! Wait a minute, Pamela . . .' but she came swiftly
across the room, right up close to me where I was standing, and
she dropped her head and looked down at me – the old look of a
smile that wasn't a smile, at the corners of the mouth, and the curl
of the nose, and the big full grey eyes staring at me with their bright
black centres, and then they were grey, and all the rest was white
flecked with hundreds of tiny red veins – and when she looked at
me like this, hard and close, I swear to you it made me feel as
though I were drowning.

'Yes,' she said. 'Why not?'

'But Pamela . . . Good heavens . . . No . . . After all . . .'

'Arthur, I do wish you wouldn't *argue* with me all the time. That's exactly what we'll do. Now, go fetch a deck of cards; we'll 5 start right away.'

# The Way up to Heaven

All her life, Mrs Foster had had an almost pathological fear of missing a train, a plane, a boat, or even a theatre curtain. In other respects, she was not a particularly nervous woman, but the mere thought of being late on occasions like these would throw her into such a state of nerves that she would begin to twitch. It was nothing much – just a tiny vellicating muscle in the corner of the left eye, like a secret wink – but the annoying thing was that it refused to disappear until an hour or so after the train or plane or whatever it was had been safely caught.

It was really extraordinary how in certain people a simple apprehension about a thing like catching a train can grow into a serious obsession. At least half an hour before it was time to leave the house for the station, Mrs Foster would step out of the elevator all ready to go, with hat and coat and gloves, and then, being quite unable to sit down, she would flutter and fidget about from room to room until her husband, who must have been well aware of her state, finally emerged from his privacy and suggested in a cool dry voice that perhaps they had better get going now, had they not?

Mr Foster may possibly have had a right to be irritated by this foolishness of his wife's, but he could have had no excuse for increasing her misery by keeping her waiting unnecessarily. Mind you, it is by no means certain that this is what he did, yet whenever they were to go somewhere, his timing was so accurate – just a minute or two late, you understand – and his manner so bland that it was hard to believe he wasn't purposely inflicting a nasty private little torture of his own on the unhappy lady. And one thing he must have known – that she would never dare to call out and tell

him to hurry. He had disciplined her too well for that. He must also have known that if he was prepared to wait even beyond the last moment of safety, he could drive her nearly into hysterics. On one or two special occasions in the later years of their married life,
5  it seemed almost as though he had *wanted* to miss the train simply in order to intensify the poor woman's suffering.

Assuming (though one cannot be sure) that the husband was guilty, what made his attitude doubly unreasonable was the fact that, with the exception of this one small irrepressible foible, Mrs
10  Foster was and always had been a good and loving wife. For over thirty years, she had served him loyally and well. There was no doubt about this. Even she, a very modest woman, was aware of it, and although she had for years refused to let herself believe that Mr Foster would ever consciously torment her, there had been
15  times recently when she had caught herself beginning to wonder.

Mr Eugene Foster, who was nearly seventy years old, lived with his wife in a large six-storey house in New York City, on East Sixty-second Street, and they had four servants. It was a gloomy place, and few people came to visit them. But on this particular
20  morning in January, the house had come alive and there was a great deal of bustling about. One maid was distributing bundles of dust sheets to every room, while another was draping them over the furniture. The butler was bringing down suitcases and putting them in the hall. The cook kept popping up from the kitchen
25  to have a word with the butler, and Mrs Foster herself, in an old-fashioned fur coat and with a black hat on the top of her head, was flying from room to room and pretending to supervise these operations. Actually, she was thinking of nothing at all except that she was going to miss her plane if her husband didn't come out of
30  his study soon and get ready.

'What time is it, Walker?' she said to the butler as she passed him.

'It's ten minutes past nine, Madam.'

'And has the car come?'

35  'Yes, Madam, it's waiting. I'm just going to put the luggage in now.'

'It takes an hour to get to Idlewild,' she said. 'My plane leaves at eleven. I have to be there half an hour beforehand for the formalities. I shall be late. I just *know* I'm going to be late.'

'I think you have plenty of time, Madam,' the butler said kindly. 'I warned Mr Foster that you must leave at nine-fifteen. There's still another five minutes.'

'Yes, Walker, I know, I know. But get the luggage in quickly, will you please?'

She began walking up and down the hall, and whenever the butler came by, she asked him the time. This, she kept telling herself, was the *one* plane she must not miss. It had taken months to persuade her husband to allow her to go. If she missed it, he might easily decide that she should cancel the whole thing. And the trouble was that he insisted on coming to the airport to see her off.

'Dear God,' she said aloud, 'I'm going to miss it. I know, I know, I *know* I'm going to miss it.' The little muscle beside the left eye was twitching madly now. The eyes themselves were very close to tears.

'What time is it, Walker?'

'It's eighteen minutes past, Madam.'

'Now I really *will* miss it!' she cried. 'Oh, I wish he would come!'

This was an important journey for Mrs Foster. She was going all alone to Paris to visit her daughter, her only child, who was married to a Frenchman. Mrs Foster didn't care much for the Frenchman, but she was fond of her daughter, and, more than that, she had developed a great yearning to set eyes on her three grandchildren. She knew them only from the many photographs that she had received and that she kept putting up all over the house. They were beautiful, these children. She doted on them, and each time a new picture arrived she would carry it away and sit with it for a long time, staring at it lovingly and searching the small faces for signs of that old satisfying blood likeness that meant so much. And now, lately, she had come more and more to feel that she did not really wish to live out her days in a place where she could not be near these children, and have them visit her, and

take them for walks, and buy them presents, and watch them grow. She knew, of course, that it was wrong and in a way disloyal to have thoughts like these while her husband was still alive. She knew also that although he was no longer active in his many enterprises,
5 he would never consent to leave New York and live in Paris. It was a miracle that he had ever agreed to let her fly over there alone for six weeks to visit them. But, oh, how she wished she could live there always, and be close to them!

'Walker, what time is it?'

10 'Twenty-two minutes past, Madam.'

As he spoke, a door opened and Mr Foster came into the hall. He stood for a moment, looking intently at his wife, and she looked back at him – at this diminutive but still quite dapper old man with the huge bearded face that bore such an astonishing resemblance
15 to those old photographs of Andrew Carnegie.

'Well,' he said, 'I suppose perhaps we'd better get going fairly soon if you want to catch that plane.'

'*Yes*, dear – *yes*! Everything's ready. The car's waiting.'

'That's good,' he said. With his head over to one side, he was
20 watching her closely. He had a peculiar way of cocking the head and then moving it in a series of small, rapid jerks. Because of this and because he was clasping his hands up high in front of him, near the chest, he was somehow like a squirrel standing there – a quick clever old squirrel from the Park.

25 'Here's Walker with your coat, dear. Put it on.'

'I'll be with you in a moment,' he said. 'I'm just going to wash my hands.'

She waited for him, and the tall butler stood beside her, holding the coat and the hat.

30 'Walker, will I miss it?'

'No, Madam,' the butler said. 'I think you'll make it all right.'

Then Mr Foster appeared again, and the butler helped him on with his coat. Mrs Foster hurried outside and got into the hired Cadillac. Her husband came after her, but he walked down the
35 steps of the house slowly, pausing halfway to observe the sky and to sniff the cold morning air.

'It looks a bit foggy,' he said as he sat down beside her in the car. 'And it's always worse out there at the airport. I shouldn't be surprised if the flight's cancelled already.'

'Don't say that, dear – *please*.'

They didn't speak again until the car had crossed over the river to Long Island.

'I arranged everything with the servants,' Mr Foster said. 'They're all going off today. I gave them half-pay for six weeks and told Walker I'd send him a telegram when we wanted them back.'

'Yes,' she said. 'He told me.'

'I'll move into the club tonight. It'll be a nice change staying at the club.'

'Yes, dear. I'll write to you.'

'I'll call in at the house occasionally to see that everything's all right and to pick up the mail.'

'But don't you really think Walker should stay there all the time to look after things?' she asked meekly.

'Nonsense. It's quite unnecessary. And anyway, I'd have to pay him full wages.'

'Oh yes,' she said. 'Of course.'

'What's more, you never know what people get up to when they're left alone in a house,' Mr Foster announced, and with that he took out a cigar and, after snipping off the end with a silver cutter, lit it with a gold lighter.

She sat still in the car with her hands clasped together tight under the rug.

'Will you write to me?' she asked.

'I'll see,' he said. 'But I doubt it. You know I don't hold with letter-writing unless there's something specific to say.'

'Yes, dear, I know. So don't you bother.'

They drove on, along Queen's Boulevard, and as they approached the flat marshland on which Idlewild is built, the fog began to thicken and the car had to slow down.

'Oh dear!' cried Mrs Foster. 'I'm *sure* I'm going to miss it now! What time is it?'

'Stop fussing,' the old man said. 'It doesn't matter anyway. It's bound to be cancelled now. They never fly in this sort of weather. I don't know why you bothered to come out.'

She couldn't be sure, but it seemed to her that there was suddenly a new note in his voice, and she turned to look at him. It was difficult to observe any change in his expression under all that hair. The mouth was what counted. She wished, as she had so often before, that she could see the mouth clearly. The eyes never showed anything except when he was in a rage.

'Of course,' he went on, 'if by any chance it *does* go, then I agree with you – you'll be certain to miss it now. Why don't you resign yourself to that?'

She turned away and peered through the window at the fog. It seemed to be getting thicker as they went along, and now she could only just make out the edge of the road and the margin of grassland beyond it. She knew that her husband was still looking at her. She glanced at him again, and this time she noticed with a kind of horror that he was staring intently at the little place in the corner of her left eye where she could feel the muscle twitching.

'Won't you?' he said.

'Won't I what?'

'Be sure to miss it now if it goes. We can't drive fast in this muck.'

He didn't speak to her any more after that. The car crawled on and on. The driver had a yellow lamp directed on to the edge of the road, and this helped him to keep going. Other lights, some white and some yellow, kept coming out of the fog towards them, and there was an especially bright one that followed close behind them all the time.

Suddenly, the driver stopped the car.

'There!' Mr Foster cried. 'We're stuck. I knew it.'

'No, sir,' the driver said, turning round. 'We made it. This is the airport.'

Without a word, Mrs Foster jumped out and hurried through the main entrance into the building. There was a mass of people inside, mostly disconsolate passengers standing around the ticket counters. She pushed her way through and spoke to the clerk.

'Yes,' he said. 'Your flight is temporarily postponed. But please don't go away. We're expecting this weather to clear any moment.'

She went back to her husband who was still sitting in the car and told him the news. 'But don't you wait, dear,' she said. 'There's no sense in that.' 5

'I won't,' he answered. 'So long as the driver can get me back. Can you get me back, driver?'

'I think so,' the man said.

'Is the luggage out?'

'Yes, sir.' 10

'Good-bye, dear,' Mrs Foster said, leaning into the car and giving her husband a small kiss on the coarse grey fur of his cheek.

'Good-bye,' he answered. 'Have a good trip.'

The car drove off, and Mrs Foster was left alone.

The rest of the day was a sort of nightmare for her. She sat for 15 hour after hour on a bench, as close to the airline counter as possible, and every thirty minutes or so she would get up and ask the clerk if the situation had changed. She always received the same reply – that she must continue to wait, because the fog might blow away at any moment. It wasn't until after six in the evening that the 20 loudspeakers finally announced that the flight had been postponed until eleven o'clock the next morning.

Mrs Foster didn't quite know what to do when she heard this news. She stayed sitting on her bench for at least another half-hour, wondering, in a tired, hazy sort of way, where she might go to 25 spend the night. She hated to leave the airport. She didn't wish to see her husband. She was terrified that in one way or another he would eventually manage to prevent her from getting to France. She would have liked to remain just where she was, sitting on the bench the whole night through. That would be the safest. But she 30 was already exhausted, and it didn't take her long to realize that this was a ridiculous thing for an elderly lady to do. So in the end she went to a phone and called the house.

Her husband, who was on the point of leaving for the club, answered it himself. She told him the news, and asked whether the 35 servants were still there.

'They've all gone,' he said.

'In that case, dear, I'll just get myself a room somewhere for the night. And don't you bother yourself about it at all.'

'That would be foolish,' he said. 'You've got a large house here
5  at your disposal. Use it.'

'But, dear, it's *empty*.'

'Then I'll stay with you myself.'

'There's no food in the house. There's nothing.'

'Then eat before you come in. Don't be so stupid, woman.
10  Everything you do, you seem to want to make a fuss about it.'

'Yes,' she said. 'I'm sorry. I'll get myself a sandwich here, and then I'll come on in.'

Outside, the fog had cleared a little, but it was still a long, slow drive in the taxi, and she didn't arrive back at the house on
15  Sixty-second Street until fairly late.

Her husband emerged from his study when he heard her coming in. 'Well,' he said, standing by the study door, 'how was Paris?'

'We leave at eleven in the morning,' she answered. 'It's definite.'

'You mean if the fog clears.'

20  'It's clearing now. There's a wind coming up.'

'You look tired,' he said. 'You must have had an anxious day.'

'It wasn't very comfortable. I think I'll go straight to bed.'

'I've ordered a car for the morning,' he said. 'Nine o'clock.'

25  'Oh, thank you, dear. And I certainly hope you're not going to bother to come all the way out again to see me off.'

'No,' he said slowly. 'I don't think I will. But there's no reason why you shouldn't drop me at the club on your way.'

She looked at him, and at that moment he seemed to be standing
30  a long way off from her, beyond some borderline. He was suddenly so small and far away that she couldn't be sure what he was doing, or what he was thinking, or even what he was.

'The club is downtown,' she said. 'It isn't on the way to the airport.'

35  'But you'll have plenty of time, my dear. Don't you want to drop me at the club?'

'Oh, yes – of course.'

'That's good. Then I'll see you in the morning at nine.'

She went up to her bedroom on the second floor, and she was so exhausted from her day that she fell asleep soon after she lay down.

Next morning, Mrs Foster was up early, and by eight-thirty she was downstairs and ready to leave.

Shortly after nine, her husband appeared. 'Did you make any coffee?' he asked.

'No, dear. I thought you'd get a nice breakfast at the club. The car is here. It's been waiting. I'm all ready to go.'

They were standing in the hall – they always seemed to be meeting in the hall nowadays – she with her hat and coat and purse, he in a curiously cut Edwardian jacket with high lapels.

'Your luggage?'

'It's at the airport.'

'Ah yes,' he said. 'Of course. And if you're going to take me to the club first, I suppose we'd better get going fairly soon, hadn't we?'

'Yes!' she cried. 'Oh, yes – *please*!'

'I'm just going to get a few cigars. I'll be right with you. You get in the car.'

She turned and went out to where the chauffeur was standing, and he opened the car door for her as she approached.

'What time is it?' she asked him.

'About nine-fifteen.'

Mr Foster came out five minutes later, and watching him as he walked slowly down the steps, she noticed that his legs were like goat's legs in those narrow stovepipe trousers that he wore. As on the day before, he paused halfway down to sniff the air and to examine the sky. The weather was still not quite clear, but there was a wisp of sun coming through the mist.

'Perhaps you'll be lucky this time,' he said as he settled himself beside her in the car.

'Hurry, please,' she said to the chauffeur. 'Don't bother about the rug. I'll arrange the rug. Please get going. I'm late.'

The man went back to his seat behind the wheel and started the engine.

'*Just* a moment!' Mr Foster said suddenly. 'Hold it a moment, chauffeur, will you?'

5 'What is it, dear?' She saw him searching the pockets of his overcoat.

'I had a little present I wanted you to take to Ellen,' he said. 'Now, where on earth is it? I'm sure I had it in my hand as I came down.'

10 'I never saw you carrying anything. What sort of present?'

'A little box wrapped up in white paper. I forgot to give it to you yesterday. I don't want to forget it today.'

'A little box!' Mrs Foster cried. 'I never saw any little box!' She began hunting frantically in the back of the car.

15 Her husband continued searching through the pockets of his coat. Then he unbuttoned the coat and felt around in his jacket. 'Confound it,' he said, 'I must've left it in my bedroom. I won't be a moment.'

'Oh, *please*!' she cried. 'We haven't got time! *Please* leave it! You 20 can mail it. It's only one of those silly combs anyway. You're always giving her combs.'

'And what's wrong with combs, may I ask?' he said, furious that she should have forgotten herself for once.

'Nothing, dear, I'm sure. But . . .'

25 'Stay here!' he commanded. 'I'm going to get it.'

'Be quick, dear! Oh, *please* be quick!'

She sat still, waiting and waiting.

'Chauffeur, what time is it?'

The man had a wristwatch, which he consulted. 'I make it nearly 30 nine-thirty.'

'Can we get to the airport in an hour?'

'Just about.'

At this point, Mrs Foster suddenly spotted a corner of something white wedged down in the crack of the seat on the side where her 35 husband had been sitting. She reached over and pulled out a small paper-wrapped box, and at the same time she couldn't help noticing that it was wedged down firm and deep, as though with the help of a pushing hand.

'Here it is!' she cried. 'I've found it! Oh dear, and now he'll be up there for ever searching for it! Chauffeur, quickly – run in and call him down, will you please?'

The chauffeur, a man with a small rebellious Irish mouth, didn't care very much for any of this, but he climbed out of the car and went up the steps to the front door of the house. Then he turned and came back. 'Door's locked,' he announced. 'You got a key?'

'Yes – wait a minute.' She began hunting madly in her purse. The little face was screwed up tight with anxiety, the lips pushed outward like a spout.

'Here it is! No – I'll go myself. It'll be quicker. I know where he'll be.'

She hurried out of the car and up the steps to the front door, holding the key in one hand. She slid the key into the keyhole and was about to turn it – and then she stopped. Her head came up, and she stood there absolutely motionless, her whole body arrested right in the middle of all this hurry to turn the key and get into the house, and she waited – five, six, seven, eight, nine, ten seconds, she waited. The way she was standing there, with her head in the air and the body so tense, it seemed as though she were listening for the repetition of some sound that she had heard a moment before from a place far away inside the house.

Yes – quite obviously she was listening. Her whole attitude was a *listening* one. She appeared actually to be moving one of her ears closer and closer to the door. Now it was right up against the door, and for still another few seconds she remained in that position, head up, ear to door, hand on key, about to enter but not entering, trying instead, or so it seemed, to hear and to analyse these sounds that were coming faintly from this place deep within the house.

Then, all at once, she sprang to life again. She withdrew the key from the door and came running back down the steps.

'It's too late!' she cried to the chauffeur. 'I can't wait for him, I simply can't. I'll miss the plane. Hurry now, driver, hurry! To the airport!'

The chauffeur, had he been watching her closely, might have noticed that her face had turned absolutely white and that the whole expression had suddenly altered. There was no longer that rather soft and silly look. A peculiar hardness had settled itself
5 upon the features. The little mouth, usually so flabby, was now tight and thin, the eyes were bright, and the voice, when she spoke, carried a new note of authority.

'Hurry, driver, hurry!'

'Isn't your husband travelling with you?' the man asked,
10 astonished.

'Certainly not! I was only going to drop him at the club. It won't matter. He'll understand. He'll get a cab. Don't sit there talking, man. *Get going!* I've got a plane to catch for Paris!'

With Mrs Foster urging him from the back seat, the man drove
15 fast all the way, and she caught her plane with a few minutes to spare. Soon she was high up over the Atlantic, reclining comfortably in her aeroplane chair, listening to the hum of the motors, heading for Paris at last. The new mood was still with her. She felt remarkably strong and, in a queer sort of way, wonderful. She was a trifle
20 breathless with it all, but this was more from pure astonishment at what she had done than anything else, and as the plane flew farther and farther away from New York and East Sixty-second Street, a great sense of calmness began to settle upon her. By the time she reached Paris, she was just as strong and cool and calm as she
25 could wish.

She met her grandchildren, and they were even more beautiful in the flesh than in their photographs. They were like angels, she told herself, so beautiful they were. And every day she took them for walks, and fed them cakes, and bought them presents, and told
30 them charming stories.

Once a week, on Tuesdays, she wrote a letter to her husband – a nice, chatty letter – full of news and gossip, which always ended with the words 'Now be sure to take your meals regularly, dear, although this is something I'm afraid you may not be doing when
35 I'm not with you.'

When the six weeks were up, everybody was sad that she had to return to America, to her husband. Everybody, that is, except her. Surprisingly, she didn't seem to mind as much as one might have expected, and when she kissed them all good-bye, there was something in her manner and in the things she said that appeared to hint at the possibility of a return in the not too distant future.

However, like the faithful wife she was, she did not overstay her time. Exactly six weeks after she had arrived, she sent a cable to her husband and caught the plane back to New York.

Arriving at Idlewild, Mrs Foster was interested to observe that there was no car to meet her. It is possible that she might even have been a little amused. But she was extremely calm and did not overtip the porter who helped her into a taxi with her baggage.

New York was colder than Paris, and there were lumps of dirty snow lying in the gutters of the streets. The taxi drew up before the house on Sixty-second Street, and Mrs Foster persuaded the driver to carry her two large cases to the top of the steps. Then she paid him off and rang the bell. She waited, but there was no answer. Just to make sure, she rang again, and she could hear it tinkling shrilly far away in the pantry, at the back of the house. But still no one came.

So she took out her own key and opened the door herself.

The first thing she saw as she entered was a great pile of mail lying on the floor where it had fallen after being slipped through the letter box. The place was dark and cold. A dust sheet was still draped over the grandfather clock. In spite of the cold, the atmosphere was peculiarly oppressive, and there was a faint and curious odour in the air that she had never smelled before.

She walked quickly across the hall and disappeared for a moment around the corner to the left, at the back. There was something deliberate and purposeful about this action; she had the air of a woman who is off to investigate a rumour or to confirm a suspicion. And when she returned a few seconds later, there was a little glimmer of satisfaction on her face.

She paused in the centre of the hall, as though wondering what to do next. Then, suddenly, she turned and went across into her husband's study. On the desk she found his address book, and

after hunting through it for a while she picked up the phone and
dialled a number.

'Hello,' she said. 'Listen – this is Nine East Sixty-second Street
. . . Yes, that's right. Could you send someone round as soon as
possible, do you think? Yes, it seems to be stuck between the second
and third floors. At least, that's where the indicator's pointing . . .
Right away? Oh, that's very kind of you. You see, my legs aren't
any too good for walking up a lot of stairs. Thank you so much.
Good-bye.'

She replaced the receiver and sat there at her husband's desk,
patiently waiting for the man who would be coming soon to repair
the lift.

# Parson's Pleasure

Mr Boggis was driving the car slowly, leaning back comfortably in
the seat with one elbow resting on the sill of the open window.
How beautiful the countryside, he thought; how pleasant to see a
sign or two of summer once again. The primroses especially. And
the hawthorn. The hawthorn was exploding white and pink and          5
red along the hedges and the primroses were growing underneath
in little clumps, and it was beautiful.

He took one hand off the wheel and lit himself a cigarette. The
best thing now, he told himself, would be to make for the top of
Brill Hill. He could see it about half a mile ahead. And that must    10
be the village of Brill, that cluster of cottages among the trees right
on the very summit. Excellent. Not many of his Sunday sections
had a nice elevation like that to work from.

He drove up the hill and stopped the car just short of the summit
on the outskirts of the village. Then he got out and looked around.    15
Down below, the countryside was spread out before him like a
huge green carpet. He could see for miles. It was perfect. He took
a pad and pencil from his pocket, leaned against the back of the
car, and allowed his practised eye to travel slowly over the landscape.

He could see one medium farmhouse over on the right, back in    20
the fields, with a track leading to it from the road. There was
another larger one beyond it. There was a house surrounded by
tall elms that looked as though it might be a Queen Anne, and
there were two likely farms away over on the left. Five places in
all. That was about the lot in this direction.                        25

Mr Boggis drew a rough sketch on his pad showing the position
of each so that he'd be able to find them easily when he was down

below, then he got back into the car and drove up through the village to the other side of the hill. From there he spotted six more possibles – five farms and one big white Georgian house. He studied the Georgian house through his binoculars. It had a clean
5  prosperous look, and the garden was well ordered. That was a pity. He ruled it out immediately. There was no point in calling on the prosperous.

In this square then, in this section, there were ten possibles in all. Ten was a nice number, Mr Boggis told himself. Just the right
10  amount for a leisurely afternoon's work. What time was it now? Twelve o'clock. He would have liked a pint of beer in the pub before he started, but on Sundays they didn't open until one. Very well, he would have it later. He glanced at the notes on his pad. He decided to take the Queen Anne first, the house with the elms.
15  It had looked nicely dilapidated through the binoculars. The people there could probably do with some money. He was always lucky with Queen Annes, anyway. Mr Boggis climbed back into the car, released the handbrake, and began cruising slowly down the hill without the engine.

20  Apart from the fact that he was at this moment disguised in the uniform of a clergyman, there was nothing very sinister about Mr Cyril Boggis. By trade he was a dealer in antique furniture, with his own shop and showroom in the King's Road, Chelsea. His premises were not large, and generally he didn't do a great deal of
25  business, but because he always bought cheap, very very cheap, and sold very very dear, he managed to make quite a tidy little income every year. He was a talented salesman, and when buying or selling a piece he could slide smoothly into whichever mood suited the client best. He could become grave and charming for
30  the aged, obsequious for the rich, sober for the godly, masterful for the weak, mischievous for the widow, arch and saucy for the spinster. He was well aware of his gift, using it shamelessly on every possible occasion; and often, at the end of an unusually good performance, it was as much as he could do to prevent himself
35  from turning aside and taking a bow or two as the thundering applause of the audience went rolling through the theatre.

In spite of this rather clownish quality of his, Mr Boggis was not a fool. In fact, it was said of him by some that he probably knew as much about French, English, and Italian furniture as anyone else in London. He also had surprisingly good taste, and he was quick to recognize and reject an ungraceful design, however genuine the article might be. His real love, naturally, was for the work of the great eighteenth-century English designers, Ince, Mayhew, Chippendale, Robert Adam, Manwaring, Inigo Jones, Hepplewhite, Kent, Johnson, George Smith, Lock, Sheraton, and the rest of them, but even with these he occasionally drew the line. He refused, for example, to allow a single piece from Chippendale's Chinese or Gothic period to come into his showroom, and the same was true of some of the heavier Italian designs of Robert Adam.

During the past few years, Mr Boggis had achieved considerable fame among his friends in the trade by his ability to produce unusual and often quite rare items with astonishing regularity. Apparently the man had a source of supply that was almost inexhaustible, a sort of private warehouse, and it seemed that all he had to do was to drive out to it once a week and help himself. Whenever they asked him where he got the stuff, he would smile knowingly and wink and murmur something about a little secret.

The idea behind Mr Boggis's little secret was a simple one, and it had come to him as a result of something that had happened on a certain Sunday afternoon nearly nine years before, while he was driving in the country.

He had gone out in the morning to visit his old mother, who lived in Sevenoaks, and on the way back the fanbelt on his car had broken, causing the engine to overheat and the water to boil away. He had got out of the car and walked to the nearest house, a smallish farm building about fifty yards off the road, and had asked the woman who answered the door if he could please have a jug of water.

While he was waiting for her to fetch it, he happened to glance in through the door to the living-room, and there, not five yards from where he was standing, he spotted something that made him so excited the sweat began to come out all over the top of his head. It was a large oak armchair of a type that he had only seen once

before in his life. Each arm, as well as the panel at the back, was supported by a row of eight beautifully turned spindles. The back panel itself was decorated by an inlay of the most delicate floral design, and the head of a duck was carved to lie along half the
5  length of either arm. Good God, he thought. This thing is late fifteenth century!

He poked his head in further through the door, and there, by heavens, was another of them on the other side of the fireplace!

He couldn't be sure, but two chairs like that must be worth at
10  least a thousand pounds up in London. And oh, what beauties they were!

When the woman returned, Mr Boggis introduced himself and straight away asked if she would like to sell her chairs.

Dear me, she said. But why on earth should she want to sell her
15  chairs?

No reason at all, except that he might be willing to give her a pretty nice price.

And how much would he give? They were definitely not for sale, but just out of curiosity, just for fun, you know, how much would
20  he give?

Thirty-five pounds.

How much?

Thirty-five pounds.

Dear me, thirty-five pounds. Well, well, that was very interesting.
25  She'd always thought they were valuable. They were very old. They were very comfortable too. She couldn't possibly do without them, not possibly. No, they were not for sale but thank you very much all the same.

They weren't really so very old, Mr Boggis told her, and they
30  wouldn't be at all easy to sell, but it just happened that he had a client who rather liked that sort of thing. Maybe he could go up another two pounds – call it thirty-seven. How about that?

They bargained for half an hour, and of course in the end Mr Boggis got the chairs and agreed to pay her something less than a
35  twentieth of their value.

That evening, driving back to London in his old station-wagon with the two fabulous chairs tucked away snugly in the back, Mr Boggis had suddenly been struck by what seemed to him to be a most remarkable idea.

Look here, he said. If there is good stuff in one farmhouse, then why not in others? Why shouldn't he search for it? Why shouldn't he comb the countryside? He could do it on Sundays. In that way, it wouldn't interfere with his work at all. He never knew what to do with his Sundays.

So Mr Boggis bought maps, large-scale maps of all the counties around London, and with a fine pen he divided each of them up into a series of squares. Each of these squares covered an actual area of five miles by five, which was about as much territory, he estimated, as he could cope with on a single Sunday, were he to comb it thoroughly. He didn't want the towns and the villages. It was the comparatively isolated places, the large farmhouses and the rather dilapidated country mansions, that he was looking for; and in this way, if he did one square each Sunday, fifty-two squares a year, he would gradually cover every farm and every country house in the home counties.

But obviously there was a bit more to it than that. Country folk are a suspicious lot. So are the impoverished rich. You can't go about ringing their bells and expecting them to show you around their houses just for the asking, because they won't do it. That way you would never get beyond the front door. How then was he to gain admittance? Perhaps it would be best if he didn't let them know he was a dealer at all. He could be the telephone man, the plumber, the gas inspector. He could even be a clergyman. . . .

From this point on, the whole scheme began to take on a more practical aspect. Mr Boggis ordered a large quantity of superior cards on which the following legend was engraved:

THE REVEREND
CYRIL WINNINGTON BOGGIS

*President of the Society
for the Preservation of
Rare Furniture*

*In association with
The Victoria and
Albert Museum*

From now on, every Sunday, he was going to be a nice old parson spending his holiday travelling around on a labour of love for the 'Society', compiling an inventory of the treasures that lay hidden in the country homes of England. And who in the world was going
5 to kick him out when they heard that one?

Nobody.

And then, once he was inside, if he happened to spot something he really wanted, well – he knew a hundred different ways of dealing with that.

10 Rather to Mr Boggis's surprise, the scheme worked. In fact, the friendliness with which he was received in one house after another through the countryside was, in the beginning, quite embarrassing, even to him. A slice of cold pie, a glass of port, a cup of tea, a basket of plums, even a full sit-down Sunday dinner with the family,
15 such things were constantly being pressed upon him. Sooner or later, of course, there had been some bad moments and a number of unpleasant incidents, but then nine years is more than four hundred Sundays, and that adds up to a great quantity of houses visited. All in all, it had been an interesting, exciting, and lucrative
20 business.

And now it was another Sunday and Mr Boggis was operating in the county of Buckinghamshire, in one of the most northerly squares on his map, about ten miles from Oxford, and as he drove down the hill and headed for his first house, the dilapidated Queen
25 Anne, he began to get the feeling that this was going to be one of his lucky days.

He parked the car about a hundred yards from the gates and got out to walk the rest of the way. He never liked people to see his car until after a deal was completed. A dear old clergyman and a
30 large station-wagon somehow never seemed quite right together. Also the short walk gave him time to examine the property closely from the outside and to assume the mood most likely to be suitable for the occasion.

Mr Boggis strode briskly up the drive. He was a small fat-legged
35 man with a belly. The face was round and rosy, quite perfect for the part, and the two large brown eyes that bulged out at you from

this rosy face gave an impression of gentle imbecility. He was dressed in a black suit with the usual parson's dog-collar round his neck, and on his head a soft black hat. He carried an old oak walking-stick which lent him, in his opinion, a rather rustic easy-going air.

He approached the front door and rang the bell. He heard the sound of footsteps in the hall and the door opened and suddenly there stood before him, or rather above him, a gigantic woman dressed in riding-breeches. Even through the smoke of her cigarette he could smell the powerful odour of stables and horse manure that clung about her.

'Yes?' she asked, looking at him suspiciously. 'What is it you want?'

Mr Boggis, who half expected her to whinny any moment, raised his hat, made a little bow, and handed her his card. 'I do apologize for bothering you,' he said, and then he waited, watching her face as she read the message.

'I don't understand,' she said, handing back the card. 'What is it you want?'

Mr Boggis explained about the Society for the Preservation of Rare Furniture.

'This wouldn't by any chance be something to do with the Socialist Party?' she asked, staring at him fiercely from under a pair of pale bushy brows.

From then on, it was easy. A Tory in riding-breeches, male or female, was always a sitting duck for Mr Boggis. He spent two minutes delivering an impassioned eulogy on the extreme Right Wing of the Conservative Party, then two more denouncing the Socialists. As a clincher, he made particular reference to the Bill that the Socialists had once introduced for the abolition of bloodsports in the country, and went on to inform his listener that his idea of heaven – 'though you better not tell the bishop, my dear' – was a place where one could hunt the fox, the stag, and the hare with large packs of tireless hounds from morn till night every day of the week, including Sundays.

Watching her as he spoke, he could see the magic beginning to do its work. The woman was grinning now, showing Mr Boggis a set of enormous, slightly yellow teeth. 'Madam,' he cried, 'I beg of you, *please* don't get me started on Socialism.' At that point, she let out a great guffaw of laughter, raised an enormous red hand, and slapped him so hard on the shoulder that he nearly went over.

'Come in!' she shouted. 'I don't know what the hell you want, but come on in!'

Unfortunately, and rather surprisingly, there was nothing of any value in the whole house, and Mr Boggis, who never wasted time on barren territory, soon made his excuses and took his leave. The whole visit had taken less than fifteen minutes, and that, he told himself as he climbed back into his car and started off for the next place, was exactly as it should be.

From now on, it was all farmhouses, and the nearest was about half a mile up the road. It was a large half-timbered brick building of considerable age, and there was a magnificent pear tree still in blossom covering almost the whole of the south wall.

Mr Boggis knocked on the door. He waited, but no one came. He knocked again, but still there was no answer, so he wandered around the back to look for the farmer among the cowsheds. There was no one there either. He guessed that they must all still be in church, so he began peering in the windows to see if he could spot anything interesting. There was nothing in the dining-room. Nothing in the library either. He tried the next window, the living-room, and there, right under his nose, in the little alcove that the window made, he saw a beautiful thing, a semicircular card-table in mahogany, richly veneered, and in the style of Hepplewhite, built around 1780.

'Ah-ha,' he said aloud, pressing his face hard against the glass. 'Well done, Boggis.'

But that was not all. There was a chair there as well, a single chair, and if he were not mistaken it was of an even finer quality than the table. Another Hepplewhite, wasn't it? And oh, what a beauty! The lattices on the back were finely carved with the honeysuckle, the husk, and the paterae, the caning on the seat was original, the legs were very gracefully turned and the two back ones had that peculiar outward splay that meant so much. It was an exquisite chair. 'Before this day is done,' Mr Boggis said softly, 'I shall have the pleasure of sitting down upon that lovely seat.' He never bought a chair without doing this. It was a favourite test of his, and it was always an intriguing sight to see him lowering himself delicately into the seat, waiting for the 'give', expertly gauging the precise but infinitesimal degree of shrinkage that the years had caused in the mortice and dovetail joints.

But there was no hurry, he told himself. He would return here later. He had the whole afternoon before him.

The next farm was situated some way back in the fields, and in order to keep his car out of sight, Mr Boggis had to leave it on the road and walk about six hundred yards along a straight track that led directly into the back yard of the farmhouse. This place, he noticed as he approached, was a good deal smaller than the last, and he didn't hold out much hope for it. It looked rambling and dirty, and some of the sheds were clearly in bad repair.

There were three men standing in a close group in a corner of the yard, and one of them had two large black greyhounds with him, on leashes. When the men caught sight of Mr Boggis walking forward in his black suit and parson's collar, they stopped talking and seemed suddenly to stiffen and freeze, becoming absolutely still, motionless, three faces turned towards him, watching him suspiciously as he approached.

The oldest of the three was a stumpy man with a wide frog-mouth and small shifty eyes, and although Mr Boggis didn't know it, his name was Rummins and he was the owner of the farm.

The tall youth beside him, who appeared to have something wrong with one eye, was Bert, the son of Rummins.

The shortish flat-faced man with a narrow corrugated brow and immensely broad shoulders was Claud. Claud had dropped in on Rummins in the hope of getting a piece of pork or ham out of him from the pig that had been killed the day before. Claud knew about the killing – the noise of it had carried far across the fields – and he also knew that a man should have a government permit to do that sort of thing, and that Rummins didn't have one.

'Good afternoon,' Mr Boggis said. 'Isn't it a lovely day?'

None of the three men moved. At that moment they were all thinking precisely the same thing – that somehow or other this clergyman, who was certainly not the local fellow, had been sent to poke his nose into their business and to report what he found to the government.

'What beautiful dogs,' Mr Boggis said. 'I must say I've never been greyhound-racing myself, but they tell me it's a fascinating sport.'

Again the silence, and Mr Boggis glanced quickly from Rummins to Bert, then to Claud, then back again to Rummins, and he noticed that each of them had the same peculiar expression on his face, something between a jeer and a challenge, with a contemptuous curl to the mouth and a sneer around the nose.

'Might I inquire if you are the owner?' Mr Boggis asked, undaunted, addressing himself to Rummins.

'What is it you want?'

'I do apologize for troubling you, especially on a Sunday.'

Mr Boggis offered his card and Rummins took it and held it up close to his face. The other two didn't move, but their eyes swivelled over to one side, trying to see.

'And what exactly might you be wanting?' Rummins asked.

For the second time that morning, Mr Boggis explained at some length the aims and ideals of the Society for the Preservation of Rare Furniture.

'We don't have any,' Rummins told him when it was over. 'You're wasting your time.'

'Now, just a minute, sir,' Mr Boggis said, raising a finger. 'The last man who said that to me was an old farmer down in Sussex, and when he finally let me into his house, d'you know what I found? A dirty-looking old chair in the corner of the kitchen, and it turned out to be worth *four hundred pounds*! I showed him how to sell it, and he bought himself a new tractor with the money.'

'What on earth are you talking about?' Claud said. 'There ain't no chair in the world worth four hundred pound.'

'Excuse me,' Mr Boggis answered primly, 'but there are plenty of chairs in England worth more than twice that figure. And you know where they are? They're tucked away in the farms and cottages all over the country, with the owners using them as steps and ladders and standing on them with hobnailed boots to reach a pot of jam out of the top cupboard or to hang a picture. This is the truth I'm telling you, my friends.'

Rummins shifted uneasily on his feet. 'You mean to say all you want to do is go inside and stand there in the middle of the room and look around?'

'Exactly,' Mr Boggis said. He was at last beginning to sense what the trouble might be. 'I don't want to pry into your cupboards or into your larder. I just want to look at the furniture to see if you happen to have any treasures here, and then I can write about them in our Society magazine.'

'You know what I think?' Rummins said, fixing him with his small wicked eyes. 'I think you're after buying the stuff yourself. Why else would you be going to all this trouble?'

'Oh, dear me. I only wish I had the money. Of course, if I saw something that I took a great fancy to, and it wasn't beyond my means, I might be tempted to make an offer. But alas, that rarely happens.'

'Well,' Rummins said, 'I don't suppose there's any harm in your taking a look around if that's all you want.' He led the way across the yard to the back door of the farmhouse, and Mr Boggis followed him; so did the son Bert, and Claud with his two dogs. They went through the kitchen, where the only furniture was a cheap deal table with a dead chicken lying on it, and they emerged into a fairly large, exceedingly filthy living-room.

And there it was! Mr Boggis saw it at once, and he stopped dead in his tracks and gave a little shrill gasp of shock. Then he stood there for five, ten, fifteen seconds at least, staring like an idiot, unable to believe, not daring to believe what he saw before him. It *couldn't* be true, not possibly! But the longer he stared, the more true it began to seem. After all, there it was standing against the wall right in front of him, as real and as solid as the house itself. And who in the world could possibly make a mistake about a thing

like that? Admittedly it was painted white, but that made not the
slightest difference. Some idiot had done that. The paint could
easily be stripped off. But good God! Just look at it! And in a place
like this!

5    At this point, Mr Boggis became aware of the three men, Rummins, Bert, and Claud, standing together in a group over by the
fireplace, watching him intently. They had seen him stop and gasp
and stare, and they must have seen his face turning red, or maybe
it was white, but in any event they had seen enough to spoil the
10  whole goddamn business if he didn't do something about it quick.
In a flash, Mr Boggis clapped one hand over his heart, staggered
to the nearest chair, and collapsed into it, breathing heavily.

    'What's the matter with you?' Claud asked.

    'It's nothing,' he gasped. 'I'll be all right in a minute. Please – a
15  glass of water. It's my heart.'

    Bert fetched him the water, handed it to him, and stayed close
beside him, staring down at him with a fatuous leer on his face.

    'I thought maybe you were looking at something,' Rummins
said. The wide frog-mouth widened a fraction further into a crafty
20  grin, showing the stubs of several broken teeth.

    'No, no,' Mr Boggis said. 'Oh dear me, no. It's just my heart.
I'm so sorry. It happens every now and then. But it goes away quite
quickly. I'll be all right in a couple of minutes.'

    He *must* have time to think, he told himself. More important
25  still, he must have time to compose himself thoroughly before he
said another word. Take it gently, Boggis. And whatever you do,
keep calm. These people may be ignorant, but they are not stupid.
They are suspicious and wary and sly. And if it is really true – no
it *can't* be, it *can't* be true . . .

30    He was holding one hand up over his eyes in a gesture of pain,
and now, very carefully, secretly, he made a little crack between
two of the fingers and peeked through.

    Sure enough, the thing was still there, and on this occasion he
took a good long look at it. Yes – he had been right the first time!
35  There wasn't the slightest doubt about it! It was really unbelievable!

    What he saw was a piece of furniture that any expert would have given almost anything to acquire. To a layman, it might not have appeared particularly impressive, especially when covered over as it was with dirty white paint, but to Mr Boggis it was a dealer's dream. He knew, as does every other dealer in Europe and America, that among the most celebrated and coveted examples of eigh- 5 teenth-century English furniture in existence are the three famous pieces known as 'The Chippendale Commodes'. He knew their history backwards – that the first was 'discovered' in 1920, in a house at Moreton-in-Marsh, and was sold at Sotheby's the same year; that the other two turned up in the same auction rooms a 10 year later, both coming out of Raynham Hall, Norfolk. They all fetched enormous prices. He couldn't quite remember the exact figure for the first one, or even the second, but he knew for certain that the last one to be sold had fetched thirty-nine hundred guineas. And that was in 1921! Today the same piece would surely be worth 15 ten thousand pounds. Some man, Mr Boggis couldn't remember his name, had made a study of these commodes fairly recently and had proved that all three must have come from the same workshop, for the veneers were all from the same log, and the same set of templates had been used in the construction of each. No invoices 20 had been found for any of them, but all the experts were agreed that these three commodes could have been executed only by Thomas Chippendale himself, with his own hands, at the most exalted period in his career.

And here, Mr Boggis kept telling himself as he peered cautiously 25 through the crack in his fingers, here was the fourth Chippendale Commode! And *he* had found it! He would be rich! He would also be famous! Each of the other three was known throughout the furniture world by a special name – The Chastleton Commode, The First Raynham Commode, The Second Raynham Commode. 30 This one would go down in history as The Boggis Commode! Just imagine the faces of the boys up there in London when they got a look at it tomorrow morning! And the luscious offers coming in from the big fellows over in the West End – Frank Partridge, Mallet, Jetley, and the rest of them! There would be a picture of it in *The* 35 *Times*, and it would say, 'The very fine Chippendale Commode which was recently discovered by Mr Cyril Boggis, a London dealer. . . .' Dear God, what a stir he was going to make!

This one here, Mr Boggis thought, was almost exactly similar to the Second Raynham Commode. (All three, the Chastleton and the two Raynhams, differed from one another in a number of small ways.) It was a most impressive handsome affair, built in the French rococo style of Chippendale's Directoire period, a kind of large fat chest-of-drawers set upon four carved and fluted legs that raised it about a foot from the ground. There were six drawers in all, two long ones in the middle and two shorter ones on either side. The serpentine front was magnificently ornamented along the top and sides and bottom, and also vertically between each set of drawers, with intricate carvings of festoons and scrolls and clusters. The brass handles, although partly obscured by white paint, appeared to be superb. It was, of course, a rather 'heavy' piece, but the design had been executed with such elegance and grace that the heaviness was in no way offensive.

'How're you feeling now?' Mr Boggis heard someone saying.

'Thank you, thank you, I'm much better already. It passes quickly. My doctor says it's nothing to worry about really so long as I rest for a few minutes whenever it happens. Ah yes,' he said, raising himself slowly to his feet. 'That's better. I'm all right now.'

A trifle unsteadily, he began to move around the room examining the furniture, one piece at a time, commenting upon it briefly. He could see at once that apart from the commode it was a very poor lot.

'Nice oak table,' he said. 'But I'm afraid it's not old enough to be of any interest. Good comfortable chairs, but quite modern, yes, quite modern. Now this cupboard, well, it's rather attractive, but again, not valuable. This chest-of-drawers' – he walked casually past the Chippendale Commode and gave it a little contemptuous flip with his fingers – 'worth a few pounds, I dare say, but no more. A rather crude reproduction, I'm afraid. Probably made in Victorian times. Did you paint it white?'

'Yes,' Rummins said, 'Bert did it.'

'A very wise move. It's considerably less offensive in white.'

'That's a strong piece of furniture,' Rummins said. 'Some nice carving on it too.'

'Machine-carved,' Mr Boggis answered superbly, bending down to examine the exquisite craftsmanship. 'You can tell it a mile off. But still, I suppose it's quite pretty in its way. It has its points.'  5

He began to saunter off, then he checked himself and turned slowly back again. He placed the tip of one finger against the point of his chin, laid his head over to one side, and frowned as though deep in thought.

'You know what?' he said, looking at the commode, speaking so  10 casually that his voice kept trailing off. 'I've just remembered . . . I've been wanting a set of legs something like that for a long time. I've got a rather curious table in my own little home, one of those low things that people put in front of the sofa, sort of a coffee-table, and last Michaelmas, when I moved house, the foolish movers  15 damaged the legs in the most shocking way. I'm very fond of that table. I always keep my big Bible on it, and all my sermon notes.'

He paused, stroking his chin with the finger. 'Now I was just thinking. These legs on your chest-of-drawers might be very suitable. Yes, they might indeed. They could easily be cut off and fixed  20 on to my table.'

He looked around and saw the three men standing absolutely still, watching him suspiciously, three pairs of eyes, all different but equally mistrusting, small pig-eyes for Rummins, large slow eyes for Claud, and two odd eyes for Bert, one of them very queer  25 and boiled and misty pale, with a little black dot in the centre, like a fish eye on a plate.

Mr Boggis smiled and shook his head. 'Come, come, what on earth am I saying? I'm talking as though I owned the piece myself. I do apologize.'  30

'What you mean to say is you'd like to buy it,' Rummins said.

'Well . . .' Mr Boggis glanced back at the commode, frowning. 'I'm not sure. I might . . . and then again . . . on second thoughts . . . no . . . I think it might be a bit too much trouble. It's not worth it. I'd better leave it.'  35

'How much were you thinking of offering?' Rummins asked.

'Not much, I'm afraid. You see, this is not a genuine antique. It's merely a reproduction.'

'I'm not so sure about that,' Rummins told him. 'It's been in *here* over twenty years, and before that it was up at the Manor
5 House. I bought it there myself at auction when the old Squire died. You can't tell me that thing's new.'

'It's not exactly new, but it's certainly not more than about sixty years old.'

'It's more than that,' Rummins said. 'Bert, where's that bit of
10 paper you once found at the back of one of them drawers? That old bill.'

The boy looked vacantly at his father.

Mr Boggis opened his mouth, then quickly shut it again without uttering a sound. He was beginning literally to shake with excite-
15 ment, and to calm himself he walked over to the window and stared out at a plump brown hen pecking around for stray grains of corn in the yard.

'It was in the back of that drawer underneath all them rabbit-snares,' Rummins was saying. 'Go on and fetch it out and show it
20 to the parson.'

When Bert went forward to the commode, Mr Boggis turned round again. He couldn't stand not watching him. He saw him pull out one of the big middle drawers, and he noticed the beautiful way in which the drawer slid open. He saw Bert's hand dipping
25 inside and rummaging around among a lot of wires and strings.

'You mean this?' Bert lifted out a piece of folded yellowing paper and carried it over to the father, who unfolded it and held it up close to his face.

'You can't tell me this writing ain't bloody old,' Rummins said,
30 and he held the paper out to Mr Boggis, whose whole arm was shaking as he took it. It was brittle and it cracked slightly between his fingers. The writing was in a long sloping copperplate hand:

Edward Montagu, Esq.          Dr

            To Thos. Chippendale
35 A large mahogany Commode Table of exceeding fine wood, very rich

carvd, set upon fluted legs, two very neat shapd long drawers in the middle part and two ditto on each side, with rich chasd Brass Handles and Ornaments, the whole completely finished in the most exquisite taste.................................................................................£87

Mr Boggis was holding on to himself tight and fighting to suppress the excitement that was spinning round inside him and making him dizzy. Oh God, it was wonderful! With the invoice, the value had climbed even higher. What in heaven's name would it fetch now? Twelve thousand pounds? Fourteen? Maybe fifteen or even twenty? Who knows?

Oh, boy!

He tossed the paper contemptuously on to the table and said quietly, 'It's exactly what I told you, a Victorian reproduction. This is simply the invoice that the seller – the man who made it and passed it off as an antique – gave to his client. I've seen lots of them. You'll notice that he doesn't say he made it himself. That would give the game away.'

'Say what you like,' Rummins announced, 'but that's an old piece of paper.'

'Of course it is, my dear friend. It's Victorian, late Victorian. About eighteen ninety. Sixty or seventy years old. I've seen hundreds of them. That was a time when masses of cabinet-makers did nothing else but apply themselves to faking the fine furniture of the century before.'

'Listen, Parson,' Rummins said, pointing at him with a thick dirty finger, 'I'm not saying as how you may not know a fair bit about this furniture business, but what I *am* saying is this: How on earth can you be so mighty sure it's a fake when you haven't even seen what it looks like underneath all that paint?'

'Come here,' Mr Boggis said. 'Come over here and I'll show you.' He stood beside the commode and waited for them to gather round. 'Now, anyone got a knife?'

Claud produced a horn-handled pocket knife, and Mr Boggis took it and opened the smallest blade. Then, working with apparent casualness but actually with extreme care, he began chipping off the white paint from a small area on the top of the commode. The paint flaked away cleanly from the old hard varnish underneath, and when he had cleared away about three square inches, he stepped back and said, 'Now, take a look at that!'

5    It was beautiful – a warm little patch of mahogany, glowing like a topaz, rich and dark with the true colour of its two hundred years.

'What's wrong with it?' Rummins asked.

'It's processed! Anyone can see that!'

'How can you see it, Mister? You tell us.'

10    'Well, I must say that's a trifle difficult to explain. It's chiefly a matter of experience. My experience tells me that without the slightest doubt this wood has been processed with lime. That's what they use for mahogany, to give it that dark aged colour. For oak, they use potash salts, and for walnut it's nitric acid, but for

15 mahogany it's always lime.'

The three men moved a little closer to peer at the wood. There was a slight stirring of interest among them now. It was always intriguing to hear about some new form of crookery or deception.

'Look closely at the grain. You see that touch of orange in among

20 the dark red-brown. That's the sign of lime.'

They leaned forward, their noses close to the wood, first Rummins, then Claud, then Bert.

'And then there's the patina,' Mr Boggis continued.

'The what?'

25    He explained to them the meaning of this word as applied to furniture.

'My dear friends, you've no idea the trouble these rascals will go to to imitate the hard beautiful bronze-like appearance of genuine patina. It's terrible, really terrible, and it makes me quite sick to

30 speak of it!' He was spitting each word sharply off the tip of the tongue and making a sour mouth to show his extreme distaste. The men waited, hoping for more secrets.

'The time and trouble that some mortals will go to in order to deceive the innocent!' Mr Boggis cried. 'It's perfectly disgusting!

35 D'you know what they did here, my friends? I can recognize it clearly. I can almost *see* them doing it, the long, complicated ritual

of rubbing the wood with linseed oil, coating it over with french polish that has been cunningly coloured, brushing it down with pumice-stone and oil, beeswaxing it with a wax that contains dirt and dust, and finally giving it the heat treatment to crack the polish so that it looks like two-hundred-year-old varnish! It really upsets 5 me to contemplate such knavery!'

The three men continued to gaze at the little patch of dark wood.

'Feel it!' Mr Boggis ordered. 'Put your fingers on it! There, how does it feel, warm or cold?'

'Feels cold,' Rummins said. 10

'Exactly, my friend! It happens to be a fact that faked patina is always cold to the touch. Real patina has a curiously warm feel to it.'

'This feels normal,' Rummins said, ready to argue.

'No, sir, it's cold. But of course it takes an experienced and 15 sensitive finger-tip to pass a positive judgement. You couldn't really be expected to judge this any more than I could be expected to judge the quality of your barley. Everything in life, my dear sir, is experience.'

The men were staring at this queer moon-faced clergyman with 20 the bulging eyes, not quite so suspiciously now because he did seem to know a bit about his subject. But they were still a long way from trusting him.

Mr Boggis bent down and pointed to one of the metal drawer-handles on the commode. 'This is another place where the fakers 25 go to work,' he said. 'Old brass normally has a colour and character all of its own. Did you know that?'

They stared at him, hoping for still more secrets.

'But the trouble is that they've become exceedingly skilled at matching it. In fact it's almost impossible to tell the difference 30 between "genuine old" and "faked old". I don't mind admitting that it has me guessing. So there's not really any point in our scraping the paint off these handles. We wouldn't be any the wiser.'

'How can you possibly make new brass look like old?' Claud 35 said. 'Brass doesn't rust, you know.'

'You are quite right, my friend. But these scoundrels have their own secret methods.'

'Such as what?' Claud asked. Any information of this nature was valuable, in his opinion. One never knew when it might come in
5  handy.

'All they have to do,' Mr Boggis said, 'is to place these handles overnight in a box of mahogany shavings saturated in sal ammoniac. The sal ammoniac turns the metal green, but if you rub off the green, you will find underneath it a fine soft silvery-warm lustre, a
10  lustre identical to that which comes with very old brass. Oh, it is so bestial, the things they do! With iron they have another trick.'

'What do they do with iron?' Claud asked, fascinated.

'Iron's easy,' Mr Boggis said. 'Iron locks and plates and hinges are simply buried in common salt and they come out all rusted
15  and pitted in no time.'

'All right,' Rummins said. 'So you admit you can't tell about the handles. For all you know, they may be hundreds and hundreds of years old. Correct?'

'Ah,' Mr Boggis whispered, fixing Rummins with two big bulging
20  brown eyes. 'That's where you're wrong. Watch this.'

From his jacket pocket, he took out a small screwdriver. At the same time, although none of them saw him do it, he also took out a little brass screw which he kept well hidden in the palm of his hand. Then he selected one of the screws in the commode – there
25  were four to each handle – and began carefully scraping all traces of white paint from its head. When he had done this, he started slowly to unscrew it.

'If this is a genuine old brass screw from the eighteenth century,' he was saying, 'the spiral will be slightly uneven and you'll be able
30  to see quite easily that it has been hand-cut with a file. But if this brasswork is faked from more recent times, Victorian or later, then obviously the screw will be of the same period. It will be a mass-produced, machine-made article. Anyone can recognize a machine-made screw. Well, we shall see.'

35  It was not difficult, as he put his hands over the old screw and drew it out, for Mr Boggis to substitute the new one hidden in his

palm. This was another little trick of his, and through the years it had proved a most rewarding one. The pockets of his clergyman's jacket were always stocked with a quantity of cheap brass screws of various sizes.

'There you are,' he said, handing the modern screw to Rummins. 5
'Take a look at that. Notice the exact evenness of the spiral? See it? Of course you do. It's just a cheap common little screw you yourself could buy today in any ironmonger's in the country.'

The screw was handed round from the one to the other, each examining it carefully. Even Rummins was impressed now. 10

Mr Boggis put the screwdriver back in his pocket together with the fine hand-cut screw that he'd taken from the commode, and then he turned and walked slowly past the three men towards the door.

'My dear friends,' he said, pausing at the entrance to the kitchen, 15
'it was so good of you to let me peep inside your little home – so kind. I do hope I haven't been a terrible old bore.'

Rummins glanced up from examining the screw. 'You didn't tell us what you were going to offer,' he said.

'Ah,' Mr Boggis said. 'That's quite right. I didn't, did I? Well, 20
to tell you the honest truth, I think it's all a bit too much trouble. I think I'll leave it.'

'How much would you give?'

'You mean that you really wish to part with it?'

'I didn't say I wished to part with it. I asked you how much.' 25

Mr Boggis looked across at the commode, and he laid his head first to one side, then to the other, and he frowned, and pushed out his lips, and shrugged his shoulders, and gave a little scornful wave of the hand as though to say the thing was hardly worth thinking about really, was it? 30

'Shall we say . . . ten pounds. I think that would be fair.'

'Ten pounds!' Rummins cried. 'Don't be so ridiculous, Parson, *please*!'

'It's worth more'n that for firewood!' Claud said, disgusted.

'Look here at the bill!' Rummins went on, stabbing that precious 35
document so fiercely with his dirty fore-finger that Mr Boggis

became alarmed. 'It tells you exactly what it cost! Eighty-seven pounds! And that's when it was new. Now it's antique it's worth double!'

'If you'll pardon me, no, sir, it's not. It's a second-hand repro-
5  duction. But I'll tell you what, my friend – I'm being rather reckless, I can't help it – I'll go up as high as fifteen pounds. How's that?'

'Make it fifty,' Rummins said.

A delicious little quiver like needles ran all the way down the back of Mr Boggis's legs and then under the soles of his feet. He
10  had it now. It was his. No question about that. But the habit of buying cheap, as cheap as it was humanly possible to buy, acquired by years of necessity and practice, was too strong in him now to permit him to give in so easily.

'My dear man,' he whispered softly, 'I only *want* the legs. Possibly
15  I could find some use for the drawers later on, but the rest of it, the carcass itself, as your friend so rightly said, it's firewood, that's all.'

'Make it thirty-five,' Rummins said.

'I *couldn't* sir, I *couldn't*! It's not worth it. And I simply mustn't
20  allow myself to haggle like this about a price. It's all wrong. I'll make you one final offer, and then I must go. Twenty pounds.'

'I'll take it,' Rummins snapped. 'It's yours.'

'Oh dear,' Mr Boggis said, clasping his hands. 'There I go again. I should never have started this in the first place.'

25  'You can't back out now, Parson. A deal's a deal.'

'Yes, yes, I know.'

'How're you going to take it?'

'Well, let me see. Perhaps if I were to drive my car up into the yard, you gentlemen would be kind enough to help me load it?'

30  'In a car? This thing'll never go in a car! You'll need a truck for this!'

'I don't think so. Anyway, we'll see. My car's on the road. I'll be back in a jiffy. We'll manage it somehow, I'm sure.'

Mr Boggis walked out into the yard and through the gate and
35  then down the long track that led across the field towards the road. He found himself giggling quite uncontrollably, and there was a

feeling inside him as though hundreds and hundreds of tiny bubbles were rising up from his stomach and bursting merrily in the top of his head, like sparkling-water. All the buttercups in the field were suddenly turning into golden sovereigns, glistening in the sunlight. The ground was littered with them, and he swung off the track on to the grass so that he could walk among them and tread on them and hear the little metallic tinkle they made as he kicked them around with his toes. He was finding it difficult to stop himself from breaking into a run. But clergymen never run; they walk slowly. Walk slowly, Boggis. Keep calm, Boggis. There's no hurry now. The commode is yours! Yours for twenty pounds, and it's worth fifteen or twenty thousand! The Boggis Commode! In ten minutes it'll be loaded into your car – it'll go in easily – and you'll be driving back to London and singing all the way! Mr Boggis driving the Boggis Commode home in the Boggis car. Historic occasion. What *wouldn't* a newspaperman give to get a picture of that! Should he arrange it? Perhaps he should. Wait and see. Oh, glorious day! Oh, lovely sunny summer day! Oh, glory be!

Back in the farmhouse, Rummins was saying, 'Fancy that old bastard giving twenty pound for a load of junk like this.'

'You did very nicely, Mr Rummins,' Claud told him. 'You think he'll pay you?'

'We don't put it in the car till he do.'

'And what if it won't go in the car?' Claud asked. 'You know what I think, Mr Rummins? You want my honest opinion? I think the bloody thing's too big to go in the car. And then what happens? Then he's going to say to hell with it and just drive off without it and you'll never see him again. Nor the money either. He didn't seem all that keen on having it, you know.'

Rummins paused to consider this new and rather alarming prospect.

'How can a thing like that possibly go in a car?' Claud went on relentlessly. 'A parson never has a big car anyway. You ever seen a parson with a big car, Mr Rummins?'

'Can't say I have.'

'Exactly! And now listen to me. I've got an idea. He told us,

didn't he, that it was only the legs he was wanting. Right? So all
we've got to do is to cut 'em off quick right here on the spot before
he comes back, then it'll be sure to go in the car. All we're doing
is saving him the trouble of cutting them off himself when he gets
5 home. How about it, Mr Rummins?' Claud's flat bovine face
glimmered with a mawkish pride.

'It's not such a bad idea at that,' Rummins said, looking at the
commode. 'In fact it's a bloody good idea. Come on then, we'll
have to hurry. You and Bert carry it out into the yard. I'll get the
10 saw. Take the drawers out first.'

Within a couple of minutes, Claud and Bert had carried the
commode outside and had laid it upside down in the yard amidst
the chicken droppings and cow dung and mud. In the distance,
half-way across the field, they could see a small black figure striding
15 along the path towards the road. They paused to watch. There was
something rather comical about the way in which this figure was
conducting itself. Every now and again it would break into a trot,
then it did a kind of hop, skip, and jump, and once it seemed as
though the sound of a cheerful song came rippling faintly to them
20 from across the meadow.

'I reckon he's balmy,' Claud said, and Bert grinned darkly, rolling
his misty eye slowly round in its socket.

Rummins came waddling over from the shed, squat and froglike,
carrying a long saw. Claud took the saw away from him and went
25 to work.

'Cut 'em close,' Rummins said. 'Don't forget he's going to use
'em on another table.'

The mahogany was hard and very dry, and as Claud worked, a
fine red dust sprayed out from the edge of the saw and fell softly to
30 the ground. One by one, the legs came off, and when they were all
severed, Bert stooped down and arranged them carefully in a row.

Claud stepped back to survey the results of his labour. There
was a longish pause.

'Just let me ask you one question, Mr Rummins,' he said slowly.
35 'Even now, could *you* put that enormous thing into the back of a
car?'

'Not unless it was a van.'

'Correct!' Claud cried. 'And parsons don't have vans, you know. All they've got usually is piddling little Morris Eights or Austin Sevens.'

'The legs is all he wants,' Rummins said. 'If the rest of it won't go in, then he can leave it. He can't complain. He's got the legs.'

'Now you know better'n that, Mr Rummins,' Claud said patiently. 'You know damn well he's going to start knocking the price if he don't get every single bit of this into the car. A parson's just as cunning as the rest of 'em when it comes to money, don't you make any mistake about that. Especially this old boy. So why don't we give him his firewood now and be done with it. Where d'you keep the axe?'

'I reckon that's fair enough,' Rummins said. 'Bert, go fetch the axe.'

Bert went into the shed and fetched a tall woodcutter's axe and gave it to Claud. Claud spat on the palms of his hands and rubbed them together. Then, with a long-armed high-swinging action, he began fiercely attacking the legless carcass of the commode.

It was hard work, and it took several minutes before he had the whole thing more or less smashed to pieces.

'I'll tell you one thing,' he said, straightening up, wiping his brow. 'That was a bloody good carpenter put this job together and I don't care what the parson says.'

'We're just in time!' Rummins called out. 'Here he comes!'

# The Sound Machine

It was a warm summer evening and Klausner walked quickly
through the front gate and around the side of the house and into
the garden at the back. He went on down the garden until he came
to a wooden shed and he unlocked the door, went inside and closed
5  the door behind him.

The interior of the shed was an unpainted room. Against one
wall, on the left, there was a long wooden workbench, and on it,
among a littering of wires and batteries and small sharp tools, there
stood a black box about three feet long, the shape of a child's coffin.
10  Klausner moved across the room to the box. The top of the box
was open, and he bent down and began to poke and peer inside it
among a mass of different-coloured wires and silver tubes. He
picked up a piece of paper that lay beside the box, studied it
carefully, put it down, peered inside the box and started running
15  his fingers along the wires, tugging gently at them to test the
connections, glancing back at the paper, then into the box, then
at the paper again, checking each wire. He did this for perhaps an
hour.

Then he put a hand around to the front of the box where there
20  were three dials, and he began to twiddle them, watching at the
same time the movement of the mechanism inside the box. All the
while he kept speaking softly to himself, nodding his head, smiling
sometimes, his hands always moving, the fingers moving swiftly,
deftly, inside the box, his mouth twisting into curious shapes when
25  a thing was delicate or difficult to do, saying, 'Yes . . . Yes . . . And
now this one . . . Yes . . . Yes. But is this right? Is it – where's my
diagram? . . . Ah, yes . . . Of course . . . Yes, yes . . . That's right

. . . And now . . . Good . . . Good . . . Yes . . . Yes, yes, yes.' His concentration was intense; his movements were quick; there was an air of urgency about the way he worked, of breathlessness, of strong suppressed excitement.

Suddenly he heard footsteps on the gravel path outside and he straightened and turned swiftly as the door opened and a tall man came in. It was Scott. It was only Scott, the Doctor.

'Well, well, well,' the Doctor said. 'So this is where you hide yourself in the evenings.'

'Hullo, Scott,' Klausner said.

'I happened to be passing,' the Doctor told him, 'so I dropped in to see how you were. There was no one in the house, so I came on down here. How's that throat of yours been behaving?'

'It's all right. It's fine.'

'Now I'm here I might as well have a look at it.'

'Please don't trouble. I'm quite cured. I'm fine.'

The Doctor began to feel the tension in the room. He looked at the black box on the bench; then he looked at the man. 'You've got your hat on,' he said.

'Oh, have I?' Klausner reached up, removed the hat and put it on the bench.

The Doctor came up closer and bent down to look into the box. 'What's this?' he said. 'Making a radio?'

'No, just fooling around.'

'It's got rather complicated looking innards.'

'Yes.' Klausner seemed tense and distracted.

'What is it?' the Doctor asked. 'It's rather a frightening-looking thing, isn't it?'

'It's just an idea.'

'Yes?'

'It has to do with sound, that's all.'

'Good heavens, man! Don't you get enough of that sort of thing all day in your work?'

'I like sound.'

'So it seems.' The Doctor went to the door, turned, and said, 'Well, I won't disturb you. Glad your throat's not worrying you any more.' But he kept standing there looking at the box, intrigued by the remarkable complexity of its inside, curious to know what this strange patient of his was up to. 'What's it really for?' he asked. 'You've made me inquisitive.'

5 Klausner looked down at the box, then at the Doctor, and he reached up and began gently to scratch the lobe of his right ear. There was a pause. The Doctor stood by the door, waiting, smiling.

'All right, I'll tell you, if you're interested.' There was another pause, and the Doctor could see that Klausner was having trouble 10 about how to begin.

He was shifting from one foot to the other, tugging at the lobe of his ear, looking at his feet, and then at last, slowly, he said, 'Well, it's like this . . . the theory is very simple really. The human ear . . . you know that it can't hear everything. There are sounds that are 15 so low-pitched or so high-pitched that it can't hear them.'

'Yes,' the Doctor said. 'Yes.'

'Well, speaking very roughly any note so high that it has more than fifteen thousand vibrations a second – we can't hear it. Dogs have better ears than us. You know you can buy a whistle whose 20 note is so high-pitched that you can't hear it at all. But a dog can hear it.'

'Yes, I've seen one,' the Doctor said.

'Of course you have. And up the scale, higher than the note of that whistle, there is another note – a vibration if you like, but I 25 prefer to think of it as a note. You can't hear that one either. And above that there is another and another rising right up the scale for ever and ever and ever, an endless succession of notes . . . an infinity of notes . . . there is a note – if only our ears could hear it – so high that it vibrates a million times a second . . . and another 30 a million times as high as that . . . and on and on, higher and higher, as far as numbers go, which is . . . infinity . . . eternity . . . beyond the stars.'

Klausner was becoming more animated every moment. He was a frail man, nervous and twitchy, with always moving hands. His 35 large head inclined towards his left shoulder as though his neck were not quite strong enough to support it rigidly. His face was smooth and pale, almost white, and the pale-grey eyes that blinked and peered from behind a pair of steel spectacles were bewildered, unfocused, remote. He was a frail, nervous, twitchy little man, a moth of a man, dreamy and distracted; suddenly fluttering and animated; and now the Doctor, looking at that strange pale face and those pale-grey eyes, felt that somehow there was about this little person a quality of distance, of immense immeasurable distance, as though the mind were far away from where the body was.

The Doctor waited for him to go on. Klausner sighed and clasped his hands tightly together. 'I believe,' he said, speaking more slowly now, 'that there is a whole world of sound about us all the time that we cannot hear. It is possible that up there in those high-pitched inaudible regions there is a new exciting music being made, with subtle harmonies and fierce grinding discords, a music so powerful that it would drive us mad if only our ears were tuned to hear the sound of it. There may be anything . . . for all we know there may –'

'Yes,' the Doctor said. 'But it's not very probable.'

'Why not? Why not?' Klausner pointed to a fly sitting on a small roll of copper wire on the workbench. 'You see that fly? What sort of noise is that fly making now? None – that one can hear. But for all we know the creature may be whistling like mad on a very high note, or barking or croaking or singing a song. It's got a mouth, hasn't it? It's got a throat?'

The Doctor looked at the fly and he smiled. He was still standing by the door with his hands on the doorknob. 'Well,' he said. 'So you're going to check up on that?'

'Some time ago,' Klausner said, 'I made a simple instrument that proved to me the existence of many odd inaudible sounds. Often I have sat and watched the needle of my instrument recording the presence of sound vibrations in the air when I myself could hear nothing. And *those* are the sounds I want to listen to. I want to know where they come from and who or what is making them.'

'And that machine on the table there,' the Doctor said, 'is that going to allow you to hear these noises?'

'It may. Who knows? So far, I've had no luck. But I've made

some changes in it and tonight I'm ready for another trial. This machine,' he said, touching it with his hands, 'is designed to pick up sound vibrations that are too high-pitched for reception by the human ear, and to convert them to a scale of audible tones. I tune
5 it in, almost like a radio.'

'How d'you mean?'

'It isn't complicated. Say I wish to listen to the squeak of a bat. That's a fairly high-pitched sound – about thirty thousand vibrations a second. The average human ear can't quite hear it.
10 Now, if there were a bat flying around this room and I tuned in to thirty thousand on my machine, I would hear the squeaking of that bat very clearly. I would even hear the correct note – F sharp, or B flat, or whatever it might be – but merely at a much *lower pitch*. Don't you understand?'

15 The Doctor looked at the long, black coffin-box. 'And you're going to try it tonight?'

'Yes.'

'Well, I wish you luck.' He glanced at his watch. 'My goodness!' he said, 'I must fly. Good-bye, and thank you for telling me. I must
20 call again sometime and find out what happened.' The Doctor went out and closed the door behind him.

For a while longer, Klausner fussed about with the wires in the black box; then he straightened up and in a soft excited whisper said, 'Now we'll try again . . . We'll take it out into the garden this
25 time . . . and then perhaps . . . perhaps . . . the reception will be better. Lift it up now . . . carefully . . . Oh, my God, it's heavy!' He carried the box to the door, found that he couldn't open the door without putting it down, carried it back, put it on the bench, opened the door, and then carried it with some difficulty into the
30 garden. He placed the box carefully on a small wooden table that stood on the lawn. He returned to the shed and fetched a pair of earphones. He plugged the wire connections from the earphones into the machine and put the earphones over his ears. The movements of his hands were quick and precise. He was excited, and
35 breathed loudly and quickly through his mouth. He kept on talking to himself with little words of comfort and encouragement, as

though he were afraid – afraid that the machine might not work and afraid also of what might happen if it did.

He stood there in the garden beside the wooden table, so pale, small, and thin that he looked like an ancient, consumptive, bespectacled child. The sun had gone down. There was no wind, no sound at all. From where he stood, he could see over a low fence into the next garden, and there was a woman walking down the garden with a flower-basket on her arm. He watched her for a while without thinking about her at all. Then he turned to the box on the table and pressed a switch on its front. He put his left hand on the volume control and his right hand on the knob that moved a needle across a large central dial, like the wavelength dial of a radio. The dial was marked with many numbers, in a series of bands, starting at 15,000 and going on up to 1,000,000.

And now he was bending forward over the machine. His head was cocked to one side in a tense, listening attitude. His right hand was beginning to turn the knob. The needle was travelling slowly across the dial, so slowly he could hardly see it move, and in the earphones he could hear a faint, spasmodic crackling.

Behind this crackling sound he could hear a distant humming tone which was the noise of the machine itself, but that was all. As he listened, he became conscious of a curious sensation, a feeling that his ears were stretching out away from his head, that each ear was connected to his head by a thin stiff wire, like a tentacle, and that the wires were lengthening, that the ears were going up and up towards a secret and forbidden territory, a dangerous ultrasonic region where ears had never been before and had no right to be.

The little needle crept slowly across the dial, and suddenly he heard a shriek, a frightful piercing shriek, and he jumped and dropped his hands, catching hold of the edge of the table. He stared around him as if expecting to see the person who had shrieked. There was no one in sight except the woman in the garden next door, and it was certainly not she. She was bending down, cutting yellow roses and putting them in her basket.

Again it came – a throatless, inhuman shriek, sharp and short, very clear and cold. The note itself possessed a minor, metallic

quality that he had never heard before. Klausner looked around him, searching instinctively for the source of the noise. The woman next door was the only living thing in sight. He saw her reach down; take a rose stem in the fingers of one hand and snip the stem with
5 a pair of scissors. Again he heard the scream.

It came at the exact moment when the rose stem was cut.

At this point, the woman straightened up, put the scissors in the basket with the roses and turned to walk away.

'Mrs Saunders!' Klausner shouted, his voice shrill with excite-
10 ment. 'Oh, Mrs Saunders!'

And looking round, the woman saw her neighbour standing on his lawn – a fantastic, arm-waving little person with a pair of earphones on his head – calling to her in a voice so high and loud that she became alarmed.

15 'Cut another one! Please cut another one quickly!'

She stood still, staring at him. 'Why, Mr Klausner,' she said. 'What's the matter?'

'Please do as I ask,' he said. 'Cut just one more rose!'

Mrs Saunders had always believed her neighbour to be a rather
20 peculiar person; now it seemed that he had gone completely crazy. She wondered whether she should run into the house and fetch her husband. No, she thought. No, he's harmless. I'll just humour him. 'Certainly, Mr Klausner, if you like,' she said. She took her scissors from the basket, bent down and snipped another rose.

25 Again Klausner heard that frightful, throatless shriek in the earphones; again it came at the exact moment the rose stem was cut. He took off the earphones and ran to the fence that separated the two gardens. 'All right,' he said. 'That's enough. No more. Please, no more.'

30 The woman stood there, a yellow rose in one hand, clippers in the other, looking at him.

'I'm going to tell you something, Mrs Saunders,' he said, 'something that you won't believe.' He put his hands on top of the fence and peered at her intently through his thick spectacles. 'You have,
35 this evening, cut a basketful of roses. You have with a sharp pair of scissors cut through the stems of living things, and each rose

that you cut screamed in the most terrible way. Did you know that, Mrs Saunders?'

'No,' she said. 'I certainly didn't know that.'

'It happens to be true,' he said. He was breathing rather rapidly, but he was trying to control his excitement. 'I heard them shrieking. Each time you cut one, I heard the cry of pain. A very high-pitched sound, approximately one hundred and thirty-two thousand vibrations a second. You couldn't possibly have heard it yourself. But *I* heard it.'

'Did you really, Mr Klausner?' She decided she would make a dash for the house in about five seconds.

'You might say,' he went on, 'that a rose bush has no nervous system to feel with, no throat to cry with. You'd be right. It hasn't. Not like ours, anyway. But *how do you know, Mrs Saunders'* – and here he leaned far over the fence and spoke in a fierce whisper – '*how do you know* that a rose bush doesn't feel as much pain when someone cuts its stem in two as you would feel if someone cut your wrist off with garden shears? *How do you know that?* It's *alive*, isn't it?'

'Yes, Mr Klausner. Oh, yes – and good night.' Quickly she turned and ran up the garden to her house. Klausner went back to the table. He put on the earphones and stood for a while listening. He could still hear the faint crackling sound and the humming noise of the machine, but nothing more. He bent down and took hold of a small white daisy growing on the lawn. He took it between thumb and forefinger and slowly pulled it upward and sideways until the stem broke.

From the moment that he started pulling to the moment when the stem broke, he heard – he distinctly heard in the earphones – a faint high-pitched cry, curiously inanimate. He took another daisy and did it again. Once more he heard the cry, but he wasn't sure now that it expressed *pain*. No, it wasn't pain; it was surprise. Or was it? It didn't really express any of the feelings or emotions known to a human being. It was just a cry, a neutral, stony cry – a single emotionless note, expressing nothing. It had been the same with the roses. He had been wrong in calling it a cry of pain. A flower probably didn't feel pain. It felt something else which we didn't know about – something called toin or spurl or plinuckment, or anything you like.

He stood up and removed the earphones. It was getting dark
5 and he could see pricks of light shining in the windows of the houses all around him. Carefully he picked up the black box from the table, carried it into the shed and put it on the workbench. Then he went out, locked the door behind him and walked up to the house.

10 The next morning Klausner was up as soon as it was light. He dressed and went straight to the shed. He picked up the machine and carried it outside, clasping it to his chest with both hands, walking unsteadily under its weight. He went past the house, out through the front gate, and across the road to the park. There he
15 paused and looked around him; then he went on until he came to a large tree, a beech tree, and he placed the machine on the ground close to the trunk of the tree. Quickly he went back to the house and got an axe from the coal cellar and carried it across the road into the park. He put the axe on the ground beside the tree. Then
20 he looked around him again, peering nervously through his thick glasses in every direction. There was no one about. It was six in the morning.

He put the earphones on his head and switched on the machine. He listened for a moment to the faint familiar humming sound;
25 then he picked up the axe, took a stance with his legs wide apart and swung the axe as hard as he could at the base of the tree trunk. The blade cut deep into the wood and stuck there, and at the instant of impact he heard a most extraordinary noise in the earphones. It was a new noise, unlike any he had heard before – a harsh, noteless,
30 enormous noise, a growling, low-pitched, screaming sound, not quick and short like the noise of the roses, but drawn out like a sob lasting for fully a minute, loudest at the moment when the axe struck, fading gradually fainter and fainter until it was gone.

Klausner stared in horror at the place where the blade of the axe
35 had sunk into the woodflesh of the tree; then gently he took the axe handle, worked the blade loose and threw the thing to the

ground. With his fingers he touched the gash that the axe had made in the wood, touching the edges of the gash, trying to press them together to close the wound, and he kept saying, 'Tree . . . oh, tree . . . I am sorry . . . I am sorry . . . but it will heal . . . it will heal fine . . .'

For a while he stood there with his hands upon the trunk of the great tree; then suddenly he turned away and hurried off out of the park, across the road, through the front gate and back into his house. He went to the telephone, consulted the book, dialled a number and waited. He held the receiver tightly in his left hand and tapped the table impatiently with his right. He heard the telephone buzzing at the other end, and then the click of a lifted receiver and a man's voice, a sleepy voice, saying: 'Hullo. Yes.'

'Dr Scott?' he said.

'Yes. Speaking.'

'Dr Scott. You must come at once – quickly, please.'

'Who is it speaking?'

'Klausner here, and you remember what I told you last night about my experience with sound, and how I hoped I might –'

'Yes, yes, of course, but what's the matter? Are you ill?'

'No, I'm not ill, but –'

'It's half-past six in the morning,' the Doctor said, 'and you call me but you are not ill.'

'Please come. Come quickly. I want someone to hear it. It's driving me mad! I can't believe it . . .'

The Doctor heard the frantic, almost hysterical note in the man's voice, the same note he was used to hearing in the voices of people who called up and said, 'There's been an accident. Come quickly.' He said slowly, 'You really want me to get out of bed and come over now?'

'Yes, now. At once, please.'

'All right, then – I'll come.'

Klausner sat down beside the telephone and waited. He tried to remember what the shriek of the tree had sounded like, but he couldn't. He could remember only that it had been enormous and frightful and that it had made him feel sick with horror. He tried

to imagine what sort of noise a human would make if he had to stand anchored to the ground while someone deliberately swung a small sharp thing at his leg so that the blade cut in deep and wedged itself in the cut. Same sort of noise perhaps? No. Quite
5 different. The noise of the tree was worse than any known human noise because of that frightening, toneless, throatless quality. He began to wonder about other living things, and he thought immediately of a field of wheat standing up straight and yellow and alive, with the mower going through it, cutting the stems, five hundred
10 stems a second, every second. Oh, my God, what would *that* noise be like? Five hundred wheat plants screaming together and every second another five hundred being cut and screaming and – no, he thought, I do not want to go to a wheat field with my machine. I would never eat bread after that. But what about potatoes and
15 cabbages and carrots and onions? And what about apples? Ah, no. Apples are all right. They fall off naturally when they are ripe. Apples are all right if you let them fall off instead of tearing them from the tree branch. But not vegetables. Not a potato for example. A potato would surely shriek; so would a carrot and an onion and
20 a cabbage . . .

He heard the click of the front-gate latch and he jumped up and went out and saw the tall Doctor coming down the patch, little black bag in hand.

'Well,' the Doctor said. 'Well, what's all the trouble?'
25 'Come with me, Doctor, I want you to hear it. I called you because you're the only one I've told. It's over the road in the park. Will you come now?'

The Doctor looked at him. He seemed calmer now. There was no sign of madness or hysteria; he was merely disturbed and excited.
30 They went across the road into the park and Klausner led the way to the great beech tree at the foot of which stood the long black coffin-box of the machine – and the axe.

'Why did you bring it out here?' the Doctor asked.

'I wanted a tree. There aren't any big trees in the garden.'
35 'And why the axe?'

'You'll see in a moment. But now please put on these earphones and listen. Listen carefully and tell me afterwards precisely what you hear. I want to make quite sure . . .'

The Doctor smiled and took the earphones and put them over his ears.

Klausner bent down and flicked the switch on the panel of the machine; then he picked up the axe and took his stance with his legs apart, ready to swing. For a moment he paused.

'Can you hear anything?' he said to the Doctor.

'Can I what?'

'Can you *hear* anything?'

'Just a humming noise.'

Klausner stood there with the axe in his hands trying to bring himself to swing, but the thought of the noise that the tree would make made him pause again.

'What are you waiting for?' the Doctor asked.

'Nothing,' Klausner answered, and then lifted the axe and swung it at the tree, and as he swung, he thought he felt, he could swear he felt a movement of the ground on which he stood. He felt a slight shifting of the earth beneath his feet as though the roots of the tree were moving underneath the soil, but it was too late to check the blow and the axe blade struck the tree and wedged deep into the wood. At that moment, high overhead, there was the cracking sound of wood splintering and the swishing sound of leaves brushing against other leaves and they both looked up and the Doctor cried, 'Watch out! Run, man! Quickly, run!'

The Doctor had ripped off the earphones and was running away fast, but Klausner stood spellbound, staring up at the great branch, sixty feet long at least, that was bending slowly downward, breaking and crackling and splintering at its thickest point, where it joined the main trunk of the tree. The branch came crashing down and Klausner leapt aside just in time. It fell upon the machine and smashed it into pieces.

'Great heavens!' shouted the Doctor as he came running back. 'That was a near one! I thought it had got you!'

Klausner was staring at the tree. His large head was leaning to one side and upon his smooth white face there was a tense, horrified expression. Slowly he walked up to the tree and gently he prised the blade loose from the trunk.

'Did you hear it?' he said, turning to the Doctor. His voice was barely audible.

The Doctor was still out of breath from running and the excitement. 'Hear what?'

'In the earphones. Did you hear anything when the axe struck?'

The Doctor began to rub the back of his neck. 'Well,' he said, 'as a matter of fact . . .' He paused and frowned and bit his lower lip. 'No, I'm not sure. I couldn't be sure. I don't suppose I had the earphones on for more than a second after the axe struck.'

'Yes, yes, but what did you hear?'

'I don't know,' the Doctor said. 'I don't know what I heard. Probably the noise of the branch breaking.' He was speaking rapidly, rather irritably.

'What did it sound like?' Klausner leaned forward slightly, staring hard at the Doctor. '*Exactly* what did it sound like?'

'Oh hell!' the Doctor said, 'I really don't know. I was more interested in getting out of the way. Let's leave it.'

'Dr Scott, *what-did-it-sound-like?*'

'For God's sake, how could I tell, what with half the tree falling on me and having to run for my life?' The Doctor certainly seemed nervous. Klausner had sensed it now. He stood quite still, staring at the Doctor and for fully half a minute he didn't speak. The Doctor moved his feet, shrugged his shoulders and half turned to go. 'Well,' he said, 'we'd better get back.'

'Look,' said the little man, and now his smooth white face became suddenly suffused with colour. 'Look,' he said, 'you stitch this up.' He pointed to the last gash that the axe had made in the tree trunk. 'You stitch this up quickly.'

'Don't be silly,' the Doctor said.

'You do as I say. Stitch it up.' Klausner was gripping the axe handle and he spoke softly, in a curious, almost a threatening tone.

'Don't be silly,' the Doctor said. 'I can't stitch through wood. Come on. Let's get back.'

'So you can't stitch through wood?'

'No, of course not.'

'Have you got any iodine in your bag?'

'What if I have?'

'Then paint the cut with iodine. It'll sting, but that can't be helped.'

'Now look,' the Doctor said, and again he turned as if to go. 'Let's not be ridiculous. Let's get back to the house and then . . .'

'*Paint-the-cut-with-iodine.*'

The Doctor hesitated. He saw Klausner's hands tightening on the handle of the axe. He decided that his only alternative was to run away fast, and he certainly wasn't going to do that.

'All right,' he said. 'I'll paint it with iodine.'

He got his black bag which was lying on the grass about ten yards away, opened it and took out a bottle of iodine and some cotton wool. He went up to the tree trunk, uncorked the bottle, tipped some of the iodine on to the cotton wool, bent down and began to dab it into the cut. He kept one eye on Klausner who was standing motionless with the axe in his hands, watching him.

'Make sure you get it right in.'

'Yes,' the Doctor said.

'Now do the other one – the one just above it!'

The Doctor did as he was told.

'There you are,' he said. 'It's done.'

He straightened up and surveyed his work in a very serious manner. 'That should do nicely.'

Klausner came closer and gravely examined the two wounds.

'Yes,' he said, nodding his huge head slowly up and down. 'Yes, that will do nicely.' He stepped back a pace. 'You'll come and look at them again tomorrow?'

'Oh, yes,' the Doctor said. 'Of course.'

'And put some more iodine on?'

'If necessary, yes.'

'Thank you, Doctor,' Klausner said, and he nodded his head again and he dropped the axe and all at once he smiled, a wild, excited smile, and quickly the Doctor went over to him and gently he took him by the arm and he said, 'Come on, we must go now,' and suddenly they were walking away, the two of them, walking silently, rather hurriedly across the park, over the road, back to the house.

# The Wish

Under the palm of one hand the child became aware of the scab 🎧
of an old cut on his kneecap. He bent forward to examine it
closely. A scab was always a fascinating thing; it presented a special
challenge he was never able to resist.

Yes, he thought, I will pick it off, even if it isn't ready, even if 5
the middle of it sticks, even if it hurts like anything.

With a fingernail he began to explore cautiously around the edges
of the scab. He got a nail underneath it, and when he raised it, but
ever so slightly, it suddenly came off, the whole hard brown scab
came off beautifully, leaving an interesting little circle of smooth 10
red skin.

Nice. Very nice indeed. He rubbed the circle and it didn't hurt.
He picked up the scab, put it on his thigh and flipped it with a
finger so that it flew away and landed on the edge of the carpet,
the enormous red and black and yellow carpet that stretched the 15
whole length of the hall from the stairs on which he sat to the front
door in the distance. A tremendous carpet. Bigger than the tennis
lawn. Much bigger than that. He regarded it gravely, setting his
eyes upon it with mild pleasure. He had never really noticed it
before, but now, all of a sudden, the colours seemed to brighten 20
mysteriously and spring out at him in a most dazzling way.

You see, he told himself, I know how it is. The red parts of the
carpet are red-hot lumps of coal. What I must do is this: I must
walk all the way along it to the front door without touching them.
If I touch the red I will be burnt. As a matter of fact, I will be burnt 25
up completely. And the black parts of the carpet . . . yes, the black
parts are snakes, poisonous snakes, adders mostly, and cobras,

131

thick like tree-trunks round the middle, and if I touch one of *them*, I'll be bitten and I'll die before tea time. And if I get across safely, without being burnt and without being bitten, I will be given a puppy for my birthday tomorrow.

5    He got to his feet and climbed higher up the stairs to obtain a better view of this vast tapestry of colour and death. Was it possible? Was there enough yellow? Yellow was the only colour he was allowed to walk on. Could it be done? This was not a journey to be undertaken lightly; the risks were far too great for that. The
10  child's face – a fringe of white-gold hair, two large blue eyes, a small pointed chin – peered down anxiously over the banisters. The yellow was a bit thin in places and there were one or two widish gaps, but it did seem to go all the way along to the other end. For someone who had only yesterday triumphantly travelled
15  the whole length of the brick path from the stables to the summer-house without touching the cracks, this carpet thing should not be too difficult. Except for the snakes. The mere thought of snakes sent a fine electricity of fear running like pins down the backs of his legs and under the soles of his feet.

20  He came slowly down the stairs and advanced to the edge of the carpet. He extended one small sandalled foot and placed it cautiously upon a patch of yellow. Then he brought the other foot up, and there was just enough room for him to stand with the two feet together. There! He had started! His bright oval face was
25  curiously intent, a shade whiter perhaps than before, and he was holding his arms out sideways to assist his balance. He took another step, lifting his foot high over a patch of black, aiming carefully with his toe for a narrow channel of yellow on the other side. When he had completed the second step he paused to rest, standing very
30  stiff and still. The narrow channel of yellow ran forward unbroken for at least five yards and he advanced gingerly along it, bit by bit, as though walking a tightrope. Where it finally curled off sideways, he had to take another long stride, this time over a vicious-looking mixture of black and red. Halfway across he began to wobble. He
35  waved his arms around wildly, windmill fashion, to keep his balance, and he got across safely and rested again on the other side. He was

quite breathless now, and so tense he stood high on his toes all the time, arms out sideways, fists clenched. He was on a big safe island of yellow. There was lots of room on it, he couldn't possibly fall off, and he stood there resting, hesitating, waiting, wishing he could stay for ever on this big safe yellow island. But the fear of not getting the puppy compelled him to go on.

Step by step, he edged further ahead, and between each one he paused to decide exactly where he should put his foot. Once, he had a choice of ways, either to left or right, and he chose the left because although it seemed the more difficult, there was not so much black in that direction. The black was what had made him nervous. He glanced quickly over his shoulder to see how far he had come. Nearly halfway. There could be no turning back now. He was in the middle and he couldn't turn back and he couldn't jump off sideways either because it was too far, and when he looked at all the red and all the black that lay ahead of him, he felt that old sudden sickening surge of panic in his chest – like last Easter time, that afternoon when he got lost all alone in the darkest part of Piper's Wood.

He took another step, placing his foot carefully upon the only little piece of yellow within reach, and this time the point of the foot came within a centimetre of some black. It wasn't touching the black, he could see it wasn't touching, he could see the small line of yellow separating the toe of his sandal from the black; but the snake stirred as though sensing his nearness, and raised its head and gazed at the foot with bright beady eyes, watching to see if it was going to touch.

'*I'm not touching you! You mustn't bite me! You know I'm not touching you!*'

Another snake slid up noiselessly beside the first, raised its head, two heads now, two pairs of eyes staring at the foot, gazing at a little naked place just below the sandal strap where the skin showed through. The child went high up on his toes and stayed there, frozen stiff with terror. It was minutes before he dared to move again.

The next step would have to be a really long one. There was this

deep curling river of black that ran clear across the width of the carpet, and he was forced by his position to cross it at its widest part. He thought first of trying to jump it, but decided he couldn't be sure of landing accurately on the narrow band of yellow on the
5  other side. He took a deep breath, lifted one foot, and inch by inch he pushed it out in front of him, far far out, then down and down until at last the tip of his sandal was across and resting safely on the edge of the yellow. He leaned forward, transferring his weight to his front foot. Then he tried to bring the back foot up as well.
10 He strained and pulled and jerked his body, but the legs were too wide apart and he couldn't make it. He tried to get back again. He couldn't do that either. He was doing the splits and he was properly stuck. He glanced down and saw this deep curling river of black underneath him. Parts of it were stirring now, and uncoiling and
15 beginning to shine with a dreadfully oily glister. He wobbled, waved his arms frantically to keep his balance, but that seemed to make it worse. He was starting to go over. He was going over to the right, quite slowly he was going over, then faster and faster, and at the last moment, instinctively he put out a hand to break the fall and
20 the next thing he saw was this bare hand of his going right into the middle of a great glistening mass of black and he gave one piercing cry as it touched.

    Outside in the sunshine, far away behind the house, the mother was looking for her son.

# Language Notes and Activities

## THE UMBRELLA MAN

### Focus

A public house or 'pub' is a place where alcoholic drinks can be bought. Pubs in town and cities are often crowded. Most pubs have a special place or small room where coats and hats and umbrellas can be put. They are not guarded. Food is also served in pubs either over the counter or in a special eating area.

There are many different types of public house. Some are large, some are small; and some are very old and are of historical importance. Some pubs have gardens where customers can sit. There are also pubs which offer entertainment and games in which customers can participate.

There used to be strict laws which governed the opening times of public houses and such laws would have applied at the time of writing the story. In 1993 these laws were relaxed and public houses may now remain open from early in the morning until 11 o'clock in the evening. Children normally have to be over 16 to enter a pub and they cannot be served with alcoholic drinks until they are 18.

In what ways might the 'umbrella man' be said to be clever?

## Follow-up

List four or five phrases used by the 'umbrella man' which show how polite he is and which help to make the mother and her daughter believe his story. For example: 'I wonder if I could ask a small favour of you' (3.25).

Write a description of the umbrella man. Refer both to his character and to his physical appearance (100 words).

Why do the mother and her daughter decide to follow the man?

What makes the 'umbrella man' appear to be 'a real gentleman'?

Why is the 'umbrella man' successful in his crime? What do you think he might do when it is not raining?

Why was the mother suspicious when the man first came up to them?

*banana split* (3.7): an ice-cream dish which normally contains layers of bananas, fruit and cream.

*chauffeur* (3.17): a person employed as a driver.

*bushy* (3.21): with thickly growing hair.

*wrinkly* (3.22): with small lines on the skin, usually the skin of an old person.

*suspicious* (3.27): thinking that something is wrong or that somebody cannot be trusted.

*pokes around* (4.3): looks around in different places.

*spot* (4.9): recognize.

*I've got myself into a bit of a scrape* (4.12): I am in a little difficulty.

*frosty-nosed* (4.17): unfriendly, cold.

*go to pieces* (4.18): become nervous and upset.

*simper* (4.20): smile in a silly or foolish way.

*didn't bat an eyelid* (4.22): showed no surprise at all.

*Not in a million years!* (6.5): Never, never, never!

*a pound note* (6.10): at the time of writing the story there were pound notes. In Britain today pound notes no longer exist: there are only pound coins.

*trickster* (6.19): someone who deceives other people.

*summing someone up* (6.28): understanding someone's character and knowing what they are like.

*dodged nimbly* (6.34): moved from side to side to avoid bumping into people, with quick and exact movements.

*bustling* (7.7): doing things in a hurried and busy way.

*pedestrians* (7.8): people who walk, go on foot.

*He's up to something* (7.10): he is planning something.

*stony-faced* (7.10): with a serious face.

*scuttling along* (7.18): moving along very quickly with short steps.

*pelting down* (7.20): raining very hard.

*brim* (7.21): edge.

*The Red Lion* (8.1): pubs in Britain have names. 'The Red Lion' is a pub. Other examples of pub names include 'The Spotted Cow', 'The Cat and the Fiddle', 'The Crown', 'The Anchor'.

*By golly* (8.20): an exclamation of surprise.

*he's got a nerve* (8.20): he's behaving badly and being rude.

*measure* (8.27): alcoholic drinks are often served in 'measures', which means units of volume.

## DIP IN THE POOL

### Focus

Cruises are trips for pleasure by ship. The trips can last a few days or can be a long holiday of several weeks. During this time the cruise liners (large passenger ships) visit many different places. On-board entertainments such as gambling and, as in this story, betting on the number of miles travelled in a day by the ship, are common.

Cruise ships are normally very luxurious and comfortable and passengers are very well looked after by stewards. Older people with a lot of money are frequent passengers on cruises. Most cruises are expensive but they offer high-quality dining and entertainment, including cinemas, nightly shows and sports. Most cruise liners have shops where expensive luxury goods can be bought.

Mr Botibol is an exception in that he does not have much money and cannot afford to lose it. While many passengers can probably afford to lose money gambling, Mr Botibol cannot afford to gamble with his money.

Notice how Mr Botibol's thoughts are described. A lot of reported speech is used and when Mr Botibol becomes very anxious we get Mr Botibol's thoughts directly, almost as if we can hear them passing quickly through his mind. For example: 'My goodness, yes . . . No problem there. And right away, yes right away, he would buy a Lincoln convertible' (14.6–10). Notice too how the title of the story is significant in its choice of words. 'Dip' has two meanings here: to take a dip means to have a swim. The meaning is, however, to have a short swim when it is safe and easy to do so; the word contrasts with the horror of drowning in a huge ocean. To have a dip into something also means to take money, sometimes when you are really not supposed to. For example, 'to dip into savings' or 'to dip into her purse'. 'Pool' also has two meanings here: the total sum of money collected as part of a card game or, as here, from gambling on the number of miles the ship travels in a day; and an area of water, as in the phrase 'swimming pool'.

Why does Mr Botibol decide to gamble?

**Follow-up**

List ten words from the story which describe Mr Botibol's range of feelings during the course of the cruise. For example, 'fear', as in 'fear assailed him' (19.24).

What does Mr Botibol say to convince himself that he should participate in the auction?

Does Mr Botibol choose a 'high field' or a 'low field' number? Why?

How do the passengers know that the weather has suddenly changed?

When Mr Botibol woke up the sea was no longer rough. Why did he want to know if the captain had made his estimate of the distance travelled by the ship?

What plan does he work out to overcome his problem?

How does he make certain that the alarm would be given when he jumped into the sea?

Do you feel sorry for Mr Botibol? Why? Why not?

Is Mr Botibol brave to jump into the sea? What else could he have done to get his money back?

Does the ending to the story surprise you? Why? Why not?

Have you ever gambled? Did you like it? Did you win? Do you think gambling is harmless or does gambling make people greedy?

*delicate* (10.2): likely to be sea-sick.
*deck steward* (10.4): a person who serves passengers on a ship.
*genial* (10.8): kind.
*assured* (10.13): calm.
*complacent* (10.13): very pleased with oneself and thinking that nothing is wrong.
*friction* (10.15): when one surface rubs all the time against another surface.
*apprehension* (10.21): fear.
*purser* (11.4): the person on a ship who looks after financial matters.
*poached turbot* (11.4): turbot is a kind of fish; poached food is cooked in gently boiling liquid.
*relish* (11.11): enjoyment.
*subsided* (11.14): became less strong and gradually stopped.
*concealed haste* (11.17): in a hurry but trying not to show it.
*his flock* (11.20): a group of people for whom he has responsibility.
*grave* (11.25): serious.
*estimate on the day's run* (11.35): a calculation of how far the ship will travel (run) in a day.
*auction pool* (11.36): an auction is the sale of something to people

who offer higher and higher prices until it is sold. For *pool*, see
'**Focus**' above.

*driving at* (12.13): trying to say.

*intent* (12.31): fixed and attentive.

*half-cocked* (12.31): at a 45 degree angle.

*half-hypnotized* (12.35): half-conscious; seeming to be half-asleep.

*hearing something straight from the horse's mouth* (13.1): being told
directly.

*welling up* (13.17): rising.

*white horses* (13.18): the waves of the sea.

*plumes of spray* (13.18): the sea blows up a spray of water like plumes
(feathers).

*slackened speed* (13.23): slowed down.

*auctioneer* (13.32): the person who is in charge of the auction.

*bills* (14.7): an American English word meaning notes of money.

*Lincoln convertible* (14.14): a Lincoln is a make of American car; a
convertible is a car with a soft roof which can be folded down.

*honey* (14.14): a word which expresses affection between men and
women.

*"low field"* . . . *"high field"* (14.25): the numbers at the lower and
higher end of the estimate.

*knocked down* (14.34): sold cheaply.

*panelling* (15.2): strips of wood which cover a wall.

*The auctioneer raised his hammer* (15.21): when the auctioneer thinks
he has the final price he raises a small hammer and says 'going
. . . going . . . gone'; he then hits his hammer on a table and the
item is sold (see 16.2).

*twenty-one hundred-odd pounds* (16.8): the word 'odd' here means
approximately.

*gratifying* (16.12): pleasing.

*contempt* (16.31): hatred.

*goddam* (16.36): a swear word which emphasizes the word which
follows.

*tapering* (17.28): narrowing.

*buttocks* (17.33): the part of the body which one sits on.

*advertent* (18.9): careful and attentive.

*suspicious* (18.16): thinking that something is wrong or that someone cannot be trusted.

*self-preservation* (18.17): making sure that one can survive.

*a cinch* (18.26): very easy.

*sharks* (19.15): very dangerous kind of fish.

*surreptitiously* (19.2): secretly and for dishonest reasons.

*rail* (19.23): a metal bar which protects people from falling.

*fear assailed him* (19.24): he became very frightened.

*propeller* (19.24): blades worked by an engine, which move a ship through water.

*belly flop* (20.1): a dive in which the whole body hits the water at the same time.

*spreadeagled* (20.15): lying with your arms and legs stretched out.

*turbulent* (20.23): rough.

*in the ship's wake* (20.23): behind the ship.

*bobbing* (20.27): moving up and down very quickly.

*speck* (20.27): small dot.

*angular* (20.31): having a clear shape with sharp points.

*horn-rimmed spectacles* (20.31): glasses with frames made of horn or plastic resembling horn.

*deliberate* (20.33): careful.

*spinsters* (20.33): women who are not married.

*tender* (21.14): gentle and caring.


# THE BUTLER

## Focus

A butler is the most important servant in a house. A butler is responsible for the running of the house and plays a part in choosing and preparing food and drink. Normally only very wealthy families can afford to employ servants, including a butler. Mr Cleaver was not born into a wealthy family but has become wealthy through business and he has already 'made a million' (a million pounds). Cleaver tries to buy himself a high social position by hiring experienced servants. The staff, however, have more distinction and more knowledge of the life styles of upper-class people than does Cleaver himself.

In this story there are two main styles of speaking. The butler speaks formal, standard English; the master speaks informal, non-standard English. Cleaver becomes linked in the reader's mind with a lower-class background. The writer suggests that the master is a member of the lower classes who has become rich. Tibbs's pronunciation and choices of grammar and vocabulary suggest that he is used to dealing with members of the upper class. It is common for servants to be addressed only by their family name (e.g. Tibbs rather than Mr Tibbs). An example of Mr Cleaver's 'lower class' speech is: 'Why don't nobody never loosen up and let themselves go?' (22.12) (in standard English this would be spoken as 'Why doesn't anybody ever loosen up and let themselves go?').

Do you think Roald Dahl creates the most sympathy for the butler or for Mr Cleaver?

**Follow-up**
How do Mr and Mrs Cleaver begin to 'climb the social ladder'?

According to Tibbs, the butler, why are the dinner parties not successful?

Why does Tibbs find it difficult to get the best wine in the world?

Why do the Cleavers' guests not appreciate the best wines?

How does Mr Cleaver make fun of his butler in front of the guests?

Is the butler right or wrong to do what he did? Why does he do it?

Is the story too short? Should we know more about the characters and the situation? Or does the length of the story give it more impact?

*climb the social ladder* (22.5): move up in society.
*lavish* (22.7): expensive and grand.
*come off* (22.8): to succeed.

*animation* (22.9): lively, interesting behaviour.

*What the heck's . . .* (22.11): What on earth . . .

*odious* (22.21): awful, hateful.

*twit* (22.22): fool.

*châteaux* (22.26): a French word meaning castles; the best wines in France are produced on estates with magnificent castles.

*flipping* (23.5): a slang word which emphasizes the word which follows.

*I don't give a hoot* (23.9): I don't care at all.

*astronomical* (23.14): very large.

*asset* (23.18): advantage.

*vigorously* (23.25): energetically.

*colossal bore* (23.28): a very boring person.

*bouquet* (23.31): pleasant smell (used with reference to wine).

*cowslips* (23.31): kind of wild flower.

*astringent* (23.32): very sharp.

*Terrific ain't it?* (23.33): an example of non-standard grammar. In standard English it would be: 'Terrific isn't it?'

*mumble* (23.34): to speak unclearly.

*twerps* (23.36): fools.

*Don't none of them appreciate . . . ?* (24.1): in standard English this would be: 'Doesn't any of them appreciate . . . ?'

*liberal* (24.8): generous.

*vinegar* (24.8): a sharp-tasting liquid.

*palate* (24.11): the top part of the inside of the mouth.

*Hogwash!* (23.13): Nonsense!

*sediment* (24.35): solid material which settles at the bottom of a liquid.

*decanted* (24.36): poured from one bottle to another.

*decanters* (25.1): bottles or jugs for serving wine.

*reverence* (25.14): respect.

*slosh* (25.16): spill.

*outraged* (25.19): very angry.

*He had caught them off balance* (25.19): He had surprised them.

# THE HITCHHIKER

## Focus

Hitchhiking is a quite common way of travelling, particularly among less well-off people in society (e.g. students, the unemployed). Several drivers are nervous about giving lifts to complete strangers. The driver of the car in this story clearly has a lot of money. The car, a BMW, is a German car with a lot of prestige and is a very expensive sports model.

The hitchhiker's dialect (non-standard English) contrasts with the driver's dialect (standard English). For example, the hitchhiker drops the 'h-' from the beginning of words and uses non-standard forms of concord between subject and verb ('that's very very 'ard to do'; 'All car-makers is liars') (28.3, 28.15). Dahl hints at class differences but the two men get on well and form a friendly relationship in which they show respect and interest in each other. In many of Dahl's stories class differences are sharper than in *The Hitchhiker*.

A 'fingersmith' is a superior kind of pickpocket. Do you approve of the hitchhiker more or less because he is so professional?

## Follow-up

Why does the writer give a lift to the hitchhiker?

What do they first talk about and why might the subject(s) be significant for the story as a whole?

What does the hitchhiker ask the driver of the car to 'prove'? Why does he do this?

What does the policeman say to the driver about his speeding?

What does the hitchhiker say to the policeman about his employment?

The driver tries to guess the hitchhiker's job. List the jobs he guesses. Why is it difficult to guess accurately?

Is the hitchhiker a criminal? Is he a good or a bad man?

How does Dahl keep the feeling of surprise in the story?

Would you give lifts to hitchhikers? What are the benefits? What are the disadvantages?

*Hitchhiker* (title): a person who travels by getting free rides in other people's vehicles. Rides are asked for by the person standing at the side of the road with his or her thumb held out.

*terrific* (26.3): a word emphasizing what follows.

*acceleration* (26.3): the rate at which the car gains speed.

*purr with pleasure* (26.10): make a quiet, continuous, vibrating sound like a contented cat.

*haymaking* (26.12): cutting grass and spreading it out to dry, before it is used for feeding animals.

*buttercups* (26.12): wild flowers.

*whispering along* (26.13): travelling silently and swiftly.

*guv'nor* (26.26): governor, a form of address used by one man to another, especially to one who is of a higher social class.

*Epsom* (27.10): a small town around forty miles south of London where there is a race-course.

*Derby Day* (27.10): the Derby is a famous horse race held every year in the second week of June at Epsom. Derby Day is the day on which this race is held.

*'em* (27.13): a shortened non-standard form of 'them'.

*lousy* (27.22): awful, horrible, poor quality.

*mugs* (27.22): fools, stupid people.

*nosy* (27.30): showing too much interest in what other people do or say.

*skilled trade* (27.33): a job for which a person has received a lot of training.

*crummy* (27.35): poor quality, unpleasant.

*'ard* (28.3): a shortened non-standard form of 'hard'.

*a tidy packet* (28.9): a lot of money.

*little job* (28.9): an informal expression used in an admiring way, describing a product.

## Language Notes and Activities

*flat out* (28.11): at top speed.

*ads* (28.16): a shortened form of 'advertisements'.

*Open 'er up* (28.18): non-standard form of 'Open her up', meaning 'Make the car go faster'.

*Don't slack off* (28.29): keep up your speed; don't go slower.

*cop* (29.1): copper, i.e. a policeman.

*Oh, my sainted aunt!* (29.4): an expression of surprise or frustration, used to emphasize what is being said.

*That's torn it!* (29.4): That's spoiled things!

*keep mum* (29.19): keep quiet, do not say anything.

*meaty* (29.21): strong, powerful.

*breeches* (29.22): trousers.

*mean as the devil* (29.27): an extremely unpleasant person.

*gob* (30.11): lump.

*'Ave* (30.18): a shortened non-standard form of 'Have'.

*offence* (30.29): an illegal act, a crime.

*fished* (31.6): searched around.

*'oo* (31.16): a shortened non-standard form of 'who'.

*bricklayer* (31.17): a person who builds walls or buildings.

*'ee* (31.17): a shortened non-standard form of 'he'.

*'andle* (31.18): a shortened non-standard form of 'handle'.

*station* (31.24): the local police office.

*for a spell* (31.35): for a period of time.

*the clink* (32.1): prison.

*hefty* (32.3): large, heavy.

*into the bargain* (32.3): an expression emphasizing the extra piece of information which has just been given.

*summons* (32.5): an order to appear in court.

*We was caught good and proper* (32.11): an example of non-standard English. In standard English it would be: 'We were caught good and proper'. Here 'good and proper' means 'thoroughly and completely'.

*solicitor* (32.15): a person who is trained to give legal advice, and sometimes represents people in court.

*whoppin'* (32.22): a shortened non-standard form of 'whopping'; enormous, very large.

*You writers really is. . .* (32.36): another example of non-standard English grammar: 'you writers really are . . .'

*nosy parkers* (32.36): people who are too interested in what other people say and do.

*And you ain't goin' to be 'appy. . .* (32.36): in standard English 'And you aren't going to be happy . . .'

*in plain clothes* (33.14): not in uniform.

*daft* (34.4): silly, stupid.

*twerp* (34.10): fool, idiot.

*titchy* (34.10): small.

*'ouse* (34.11): a shortened non-standard form of 'house'.

*ain't it?* (34.12): in standard English 'isn't it?'

*'Ow* (34.15): a shortened non-standard form of 'How'.

*darn* (34.17): a word used to emphasize the word which follows.

*conjuring tricks* (34.18): tricks where something is made to appear as if by magic.

*conjuror* (34.19): a person who does magic tricks.

*makin' rabbits come out of top 'ats* (34.21): a typical magic trick is to make a rabbit appear from a supposedly empty top hat.

*cardsharper* (34.24): a person who earns money by cheating when playing cards.

*racket* (34.24): a dishonest activity that is used to make money.

*give up* (34.26): stop trying to guess.

*running down* (34.29): travelling down.

*buckle* (34.33): a piece of metal at the end of a belt which is used to fasten it.

*flabbergasted* (35.5): very surprised or shocked.

*shoelace* (35.13): narrow pieces of stringlike material used to fasten shoes.

*Good grief!* (35.19): an expression of surprise, used to emphasize what is being said.

*You never saw nothin'* (35.21): in standard English, 'You didn't see anything' or 'You saw nothing'.

*homemade* (35.25): made by oneself, not mass produced or bought from a shop.

*Nice bit of stuff, this* (35.36): an informal expression meaning a desirable item.

*quality goods* (36.1): items of a high standard.

*huffily* (36.3): in an offended or annoyed way.

*pal* (36.6): friend.

*lift* (36.6): a free ride in someone else's car.

*stubby* (36.14): short and thick.

*jeweller* (36.17): a person who makes, sells and repairs jewellery and watches.

*eighteenth century* (36.19): made in the eighteenth century, that is between 1700 and 1799.

*pickpocket* (36.23): a thief who steals out of pockets and bags, especially in a crowded area.

*Pickpockets is coarse and vulgar* (36.25): in standard English, 'Pickpockets are coarse and vulgar'.

*amateur* (36.26): not professional.

*President of the Royal College of Surgeons* (36.30): the person who holds the highest position in the governing body of doctors.

*Archbishop of Canterbury* (36.30): the person who holds the highest position in the Church of England.

*Race meetings is easy meat* (37.4): the hitchhiker is suggesting that it is not difficult to pick people's pockets at race meetings.

*you simply follows after 'im and 'elps yourself* (37.7): in standard English, 'you simply follow him and help yourself'.

*don't get me wrong* (37.7): don't misunderstand me.

*I never takes nothin'. . .* (37.8): in standard English, 'I never take anything . . .'

*a loser* (37.8): a person who never wins anything, or is never successful at anything.

*I only go after them as can afford it* (37.9): here, to go after means to choose. This is also non-standard grammar. In standard English, it would be: 'I only go after those who can afford it'.

*'ee ain't got it all written down* (37.29): another example of non-standard grammar. In standard English, it would be 'he hasn't got it all written down'.

*decent* (37.3): good.

*delicate* (38.1): narrow, graceful.

*brilliant* (38.9): extremely clever.

*bonfire* (38.11): a small fire that is made outside, usually to burn rubbish.

# MR BOTIBOL

## Focus

Even though he believes he is not successful, Mr Botibol is wealthy and can afford to have servants. He owns a large house and the house has rooms which are large enough for him to pretend to hold concerts in them. Mr Botibol is very knowledgeable about music and is well acquainted with the great classical composers.

Notice that the character has the same name as the main character in 'Dip in the Pool'. This is of course not the same character, but Roald Dahl obviously liked the name.

'I . . . cannot remember having had a single success of any sort during my whole life' (42.15). Do you think Mr Botibol's life has been a failure?

## Follow-up

Why does Mr Botibol meet Mr Clements and how much alcohol did they drink?

What does Mr Botibol say to Mr Clements about his life?

What does Mr Botibol hear on the radio when he reaches home?

What does Mr Botibol invite Miss Darlington to do? Why does he invite her?

What did Mr Botibol and Miss Darlington do at the end of the performance?

What is Miss Darlington's job? What is the significance of this?

Do you think Mr Botibol is a nice man? Would you like to meet him? What do you think of Miss Darlington?

**Language Notes and Activities**

Have you ever dreamt of being a great writer or composer or artist?

Do you think the events of the story are *too* unreal and impossible? Is Mr Botibol's imagination too strong?

What do you think of the story? How unusual do you think it is? Say what you like or don't like about the story.

*foyer* (39.2): entrance hall.

*self-effacing* (39.13): not drawing attention to oneself.

*conspicuous* (39.15): easily noticed.

*asparagus* (39.16): a vegetable with long, pale green, juicy stems.

*double-breasted suit* (39.20): a suit whose jacket has two wide sections at the front which overlap when fastened up.

*accentuated* (39.21): emphasized.

*preposterous* (39.21): very foolish, ridiculous.

*sole* (40.2): only.

*exploratory* (40.3): made in order to discover or learn about something.

*banter* (40.16): lighthearted, teasing, joking talk.

*it's on me* (40.24): I will pay.

*roast partridges* (40.30): a partridge is a small bird. When food is roasted, it is cooked in an oven, in a dry heat.

*commission* (40.31): a payment made to someone for selling something, directly related to the value of the goods sold.

*touching on* (40.34): finding.

*estimated* (41.10): guessed, or judged.

*old boy* (41.18): an old-fashioned form of address used especially by men of the middle and upper classes.

*to figure* (42.1): to work out.

*the wine has gone a little to my head* (42.4): the wine has made me slightly drunk.

*one hell of. . .* (42.20): an expression which emphasizes what follows.

*quota* (42.26): fixed amount.

*goddammit* (42.27): a swear word used for emphasis, expressing anger or surprise.

*making some runs* (42.29): this refers to the sport of cricket. In cricket, a run is a single point scored by running between marked points on the pitch.

*exasperated* (42.33): frustrated, extremely annoyed or disappointed.

*down-and-out tramp* (43.16): a person without a home, a job or money.

*within striking distance* (43.28): close to, near to.

*giddy* (44.3): dizzy, feeling as if one is about to fall over.

*solicitor* (44.4): a person trained to give legal advice.

*casual* (44.9): not regular or permanent.

*tipsy* (44.12): slightly drunk.

*rostrum* (44.20): a raised platform.

*white tie and tails* (44.20): formal evening dress.

*baton* (44.24): a light, thin stick.

*reverence* (44.24): a feeling of great admiration or respect.

*enraptured* (44.26): filled with great pleasure.

*majestically* (44.28): with great beauty or power.

*clenching* (44.29): squeezing, closing very tightly.

*they could hardly stand it* (44.31): they could scarcely bear or endure it.

*carried away* (44.32): very excited; with his feelings or emotions out of control.

*conductor* (44.33): a person who directs a group of people playing music, by standing in front of them and making gestures with his or her arms.

*anticipate* (45.5): know in advance that something is coming.

*tempo* (45.5): the speed or rhythm of a piece of music.

*immobile* (45.10): still, not moving.

*swelled* (45.11): became louder.

*frenzied* (45.12): wild, excited, uncontrolled.

*chords* (45.15): several musical notes played at the same time.

*Phew!* (45.19): an exclamation expressing relief.

*My goodness gracious me* (45.19): a phrase used to express surprise.

*exhilarated* (45.23): very excited.

*in retrospect* (45.28): looking back.

*downright* (45.30): a word emphasizing the word that follows.

*Letting himself go* (45.31): Losing control of himself.

## Language Notes and Activities

*furtively* (45.36): in a secretive way.

*retiring* (46.10): shy and tending to avoid other people.

*He was his own master* (46.28): he was independent, able to make his own decisions.

*to hell with. . .* (46.30): an expression meaning that one does not care about something or someone.

*give a damn about* (46.34): did not care about at all.

*preliminaries* (47.15): introductions, something that comes before the main event.

*gramophone* (47.18): an old word for record player or hi-fi system.

*impressive* (47.30): very striking or admirable.

*exultation* (47.31): great happiness or pleasure.

*solar plexus* (47.33): the part of the stomach just below the ribs.

*by heavens* (48.12): an expression used to emphasize what is being said.

*a firm of decorators* (48.13): a business which employs people to paint and decorate rooms.

*miniature* (48.14): a smaller version of something.

*plush* (48.16): a type of fabric with a thick, soft surface.

*self-changing gramophone* (48.20): a type of record player that changes records by itself.

*amplifiers* (48.20): devices that make sounds louder.

*auditorium* (48.21): a part of a theatre or concert hall where those who come to watch or listen sit.

*a place which specialized in . . .* (48.23): a firm whose main products were . . .

*damn well* (49.1): an expression used to emphasize what follows.

*masterpiece* (49.27): an extremely good piece of work.

*wave of clapping* (49.31): a sudden increase of clapping, spreading throughout the audience.

*ovation* (49.36): loud and long clapping.

*encore!* (50.9): people shout *encore!* at the end of a performance when they want the performer to play or sing again.

*he didn't want anything to break the spell* (50.17): he did not want to return to reality.

*choral* (50.32): music sung by a group of people or choir.

*recitals* (51.8): performance of music, or poetry.

*Bechsteins and Steinways* (51.9): types of piano.

*snatches* (51.11): small pieces.

*chute* (51.14): a tube or passage down which things are dropped.

*Nocturnes* (51.18): short, gentle pieces of music.

*Études* (51.19): short pieces of music written for one instrument.

*Waltzes* (51.19): pieces of music with a rhythm of three beats in each bar.

*concert grand* (51.26): the largest size of piano.

*It gives me a kick* (51.34): It gives me a feeling of great pleasure or excitement.

*you ought to be locked up* (52.4): an expression suggesting that someone is behaving in an unreasonable or insane way, and therefore they should be locked away from society.

*squat* (52.20): short and thick.

*dirty old men* (53.7): an expression sometimes used about old or older men who have an unpleasant interest in sex and in young or younger women.

*stumpy* (53.27): short and thick.

*brooding* (53.34): thinking about things for a long time which are worrying, sad or annoying.

*trepidation* (54.7): fear or anxiety.

*My goodness!* (55.3): an expression of surprise.

*a trifle sheepish* (56.20): slightly foolish, looking as if he had done something silly.

*worked up* (56.22): in a state of excitement or anger.

*It'll be a bit of a lark* (56.28): It will be fun.

*Horowitz* (57.15): a world-famous pianist.

*distinguished* (58.8): stylish, grand.

*mantelpiece* (60.4): the top part of the surrounding frame for a fire, usually made from wood or stone.

*Schnabel* (60.18): a world-famous pianist.

# MY LADY LOVE, MY DOVE

## Focus

Pamela and Arthur are wealthy. They live in a large house with extensive gardens and a gardener who looks after the gardens. The author points out, however, that much of the money is Pamela's. The Snapes are their weekend guests and they plan to try to trick Arthur and Pamela in order to take money from them.

Bridge is a card game for four people playing in pairs, often played by upper-class people. To be successful it is necessary to have a good memory of the cards which have been played. Bridge is often played for 'stakes' and large sums of money can be won even when the game is played, as it is here, between social guests.

The story is a first-person narrative. The author gives us Arthur's thoughts directly, particularly when he is weighing things up in his mind. For example: 'My wife's house. Her garden. How beautiful it all was!' (63.22). Also significant is Pamela's use of language to bully her husband and to show herself in control of situations. For example: 'Don't be such a pompous hypocrite . . . What on earth's come over you?' (65.25); 'Come on, Arthur. Don't be so flabby' (66.24).

'But listen, Arthur. I'm a *nasty* person. And so are you – in a secret sort of way. That's why we get along together' (65.29). Do you agree that Arthur and Pamela are equally 'nasty' people? If so, how are they nasty?

## Follow-up

Why is Pamela not looking forward to the weekend?

What do Arthur and Pamela not like about the Snapes?

What do they decide to do with a microphone?

Why does it take a long time to put a microphone in the guest's room?

What is a 'bidding code' and why do the Snapes use it?

What do Arthur and Pamela decide to do after they hear the Snapes talking?

Should Arthur and Pamela have openly accused the Snapes of cheating? If so, why? If not, why not?

Do you think that Arthur is dominated by Pamela?

Have you ever spent time with people you do not particularly like? How did you decide to liven things up?

*My Dove* (title): a term of affection; a dove is a kind of white bird. It is often associated with love.

*a nap* (61.1): a short sleep.

*drop off* (61.4): go to sleep.

*Doubleday and Westwood's 'The Genera of Diurnal Lepidoptera'* (61.7): a book about butterflies.

*sofa* (61.9): a long, comfortable seat with a back and two arms, on which two or three people can sit.

*They're absolutely the end* (62.2): an expression meaning that Pamela dislikes them very much.

*embroidery* (62.9): sewing designs onto cloth.

*glimmer* (62.11): shine, glow.

*with that compressed acid look* (62.13): with an expression on one's face which looks as if one has tasted something bitter.

*petulant* (62.14): bad-tempered.

*stately* (62.16): grand.

*A pair of stupid climbers* (62.29): two people foolishly trying to move up into a higher social class.

*playing with rabbits* (62.35): playing with timid, frightened people.

*for God's sake* (63.4): a phrase used for emphasis, expressing anger or impatience.

*pompous* (63.8): serious; in a self-important manner.

*french windows* (63.11): glass doors which lead out into a garden.

*laburnums* (63.14): a kind of tree.

## Language Notes and Activities

*herbaceous border* (63.16): a piece of ground in a garden containing plants which flower year after year.

*hybrid lupins . . . iris* (63.17): types of flowers grown in a garden.

*less solicitous of my welfare* (63.23): less concerned about my state of health and happiness.

*prone* (63.24): likely.

*coax* (63.24): persuade.

*everything would be heaven* (63.25): everything would be perfect.

*I am not the captain of my ship* (63.28): I am not in control of my own affairs.

*a trifle irritating* (63.29): slightly annoying.

*mannerisms* (63.30): particular and continual ways of behaving and speaking.

*intimidate* (63.34): frighten in order to make someone do something.

*an overbearing woman* (63.35): a woman who tries to make other people do what she wants by behaving in an unpleasant and forceful way.

*ass* (64.19): fool, a stupid person.

*recklessness* (64.21): lack of care about danger or the results of one's actions.

*microphone* (64.28): a device for transmitting sounds or recording onto a tape recorder. A 'mike' (66.28) is a shortened version of the word.

*assert* (65.3): act in a forceful way in order to show authority.

*What in God's name. . .* (65.6): an expression used to add force to what is being said.

*Tommyrot!* (65.10): Nonsense!

*contemptuous manner* (65.24): in a way which expresses dislike and a lack of respect.

*hypocrite* (65.25): a person who pretends to have beliefs and standards that he or she does not really have.

*reform* (65.35): become a better person, improve one's behaviour.

*a stinker* (66.3): an unpleasant person.

*stuffy* (66.13): dull, boring.

*purse* (66.16): in American English, a handbag. In British English a purse is a small bag in which money, especially coins, is carried.

*flabby* (66.25): weak, not strong or firm.

*caught red-handed* (66.33): discovered in the act of doing something wrong.

*My God!* (67.10): an exclamation of surprise or anger.

*at the very prospect* (67.11): at the thought of something that is going to happen.

*hesitated* (67.14): paused slightly before doing something.

*resigned* (67.18): accepting the situation.

*queue* (67.19): a line of people waiting for something.

*Good heavens* (67.29): an expression of surprise or emphasizing the words which follow.

*collar stud* (68.8): a small button-like object used to fasten the detached collar of a shirt.

*springing* (68.9): the coiled wires which form the insides of certain pieces of furniture such as sofas and armchairs.

*gravel* (68.21): small stones.

*frantically* (68.32): in a wild and desperate way.

*unobtrusively* (68.36): without being noticed or seen.

*elementary* (69.1): simple.

*to compose myself* (69.15): try to seem calm and in control.

*with the blood, as it were, still wet on my hands* (69.16): when people are said to have blood on their hands, it means that they have been caught in the act of doing something wrong.

*'Vanessa cardui' – the 'painted lady'* (69.18): a type of butterfly.

*a paper* (69.19): an article or essay.

*grave* (69.22): serious.

*attentive* (69.22): alert.

*breeding* (70.16): coming from a good or upper-class family.

*supercilious* (70.20): act in a scornful way as if one is better than other people.

*omniscient* (70.20): knowing or seeming to know everything.

*preoccupation* (70.22): something a person keeps thinking about because it is important to them.

*mop of black hair* (70.25): a large amount of loose or untidy hair.

*jokes, but they were on a high level* (70.27): the jokes were not rude or offensive.

## Language Notes and Activities

*Eton* (70.35): a famous (and very expensive) English private school.

*bosom* (71.1): an old word for a woman's breasts.

*resignation* (71.23): accepting a situation.

*droll* (71.27): amusing.

*Richebourg '34* (71.28): a type of wine.

*cold feet* (71.35): afraid or nervous about doing something.

*to relish the prospect* (71.36): to look forward to something very much.

*covert* (72.1): hidden, secret.

*Heaven knows* (72.9): an exclamation used for emphasis.

*gloating* (72.17): pleased with one's own success.

*momentary* (72.22): lasting only for a few seconds.

*rubber* (72.28): a series of games in bridge.

*She herded us out* (72.31): She moved us out.

*maid* (72.34): a female servant.

*skirting* (73.3): a narrow piece of wood which goes along the bottom of the walls in a room and makes a border between the walls and the floor.

*conspicuous* (73.4): easily noticed.

*craned* (73.17): stretched.

*goddam* (73.21): a swear word which emphasizes the word which follows.

*bloody* (73.23): a swear word which emphasizes the word which follows.

*bitch* (73.35): a rude and offensive way to refer to a woman.

*I'll sing them out* (74.3): I'll shout them out.

*lilting* (74.20): rising and falling in pitch.

*My heaven's alive!* (74.34): a phrase expressing surprise.

*blindfold* (75.2): with a strip of cloth tied over the eyes, so that a person is unable to see.

*flecked* (75.34): covered with.

*I swear to you* (75.35): an expression used to emphasize the fact that the truth is being told.

*deck of cards* (76.4): a pack of playing cards.

# THE WAY UP TO HEAVEN

## Focus

The story is set in New York. Mr and Mrs Foster are obviously wealthy as they have four servants. They also have a large six-storey house which would be very expensive to buy in such a city. It is common for a house with so many storeys to have a lift.

New York City, like many major cities in the world, has many traffic jams. It therefore takes a long time to get from the centre of the city to the airport. Fogs are common in the winter and flights are often delayed.

In this story Roald Dahl excels in creating tension. One particular moment is when Mrs Foster leaves her house for the airport a second time: 'She slid the key into the keyhole and was about to turn it – and then she stopped . . . and she waited – five, six, seven, eight, nine, ten seconds, she waited . . . Then, all at once, she sprang to life again. She withdrew the key from the door and came running back down the steps' (87.16–33).

What are Mrs Foster's feelings at the end of the story?

## Follow-up

Why is Mrs Foster so nervous and anxious at the start of the story? Why is she upset with her husband?

Why does she return home when the flight is postponed?

How does her husband make her anxious the following morning?

What crucial decision does she finally make?

How did she feel about being in Paris and why?

What does the following phrase tell us: 'there was a faint and curious odour in the air that she had never smelled before' (89.26?) What happened to Mr Foster?

Is Mrs Foster right to want to live in Paris? Should husbands and wives always go away together?

Do you think Mr Foster was right to say to his wife: 'Everything you do, you seem to want to make a fuss about it' (84.10)? Why do you think he says it?

Is the ending to the story predictable or unpredictable? Give reasons.

Would the story be better if we knew what happened in the end to Mrs Foster?

*pathological fear* (77.1): pathological is used to describe people who act in an extreme way and are not able to easily control themselves.

*theatre curtain* (77.2): the start of a play when the curtains are first opened.

*vellicating* (77.6): twitching.

*wink* (77.7): close one eye very briefly.

*apprehension* (77.10): a feeling that something awful might happen.

*obsession* (77.12): something about which a person cannot stop thinking.

*elevator* (77.13): a device which carries people from floor to floor in a building so that they do not have to climb the stairs. 'Elevator' is an American English word; the British English word is 'lift'. In this story the author uses both words (e.g. 90.12).

*flutter* (77.15): move lightly and quickly.

*fidget* (77.15): make constant small movements in an annoying way.

*misery* (77.21): great discomfort or suffering.

*bland* (77.24): mild, gentle.

*inflicting* (77.25): making someone suffer something unpleasant.

*disciplined* (78.1): controlled, trained to behave in a certain way.

*hysterics* (78.3): in a state of extreme panic, anger or excitement.

*intensify* (78.6): become greater in strength.

*irrepressible* (78.9): unable to be held back or controlled.

*foible* (78.9): a habit or tendency that is rather odd or silly.

*torment* (78.14): to cause extreme pain or unhappiness.

*maid* (78.21): a female servant.

*dust sheets* (78.22): pieces of cloth used to cover furniture if it is not to be used for some time, or if the room is to be decorated.

*butler* (78.23): the most important male servant in the house.

*old-fashioned* (78.26): out of date, not modern.

*Idlewild* (79.1): former name of New York's main airport.

*formalities* (79.3): official actions or processes which have to be completed in a particular situation.

*Dear God* (79.16): an expression used to emphasize what is being said.

*yearning* (79.27): a strong desire.

*doted on* (79.30): loved very much.

*blood likeness* (79.33): family resemblance; looking as if they were members of the same family.

*enterprises* (80.4): business affairs.

*miracle* (80.6): a wonderful and surprising event.

*diminutive* (80.13): very small.

*dapper* (80.13): neat, small and slim.

*bore . . . resemblance* (80.14): looked like.

*cocking the head* (80.20): moving his head at an angle.

*club* (81.11): a place where elected members, usually male, meet together, have meals or stay for a short period of time.

*occasionally* (81.14): from time to time.

*rug* (81.26): a large piece of warm fabric used to cover over the legs.

*fussing* (81.36): behaving in a worried or nervous way.

*in this muck* (82.21): in this awful, filthy weather.

*crawled* (82.23): moved very slowly.

*disconsolate* (82.35): unhappy, disappointed.

*temporarily* (83.1): for a short time.

*postponed* (83.1): arranged to take place later.

*a sort of a nightmare* (83.15): like a very frightening dream.

*exhausted* (83.31): very tired.

*at your disposal* (84.5): able to be used at any time for any purpose.

*anxious* (84.21): worrying.

*downtown* (84.33): in or near to the centre of a large town or city.

*a curiously cut Edwardian jacket* (85.14): an odd-looking jacket that looks as if it was made in the early years of the twentieth century (at the time of King Edward VII, 1901–10).

*lapels* (85.14): cloth at the front of a jacket which folds back at the top of each edge.

*chauffeur* (85.23): a servant who drives the car.

*stovepipe trousers* (85.29): trousers with narrow legs.

*overcoat* (86.6): a thick, warm coat worn in winter.

*present* (86.7): something which is given to someone else, a gift.

*Confound it* (86.17): an exclamation of annoyance or irritation.

*a small rebellious Irish mouth* (87.6): a phrase suggesting that the man did not like being told what to do, and this was shown in the expression on his face.

*arrested* (87.18): stopped.

*repetition* (87.23): something that happens again.

*flabby* (88.5): slack, loose.

*reclining* (88.16): sitting back at an angle.

*in the flesh* (88.27): in reality, as they actually are, not just as they appear to be in a photograph.

*chatty* (88.32): friendly, informal.

*gossip* (88.32): casual news.

*cable* (89.7): a message sent by electric signal.

*pantry* (89.19): a small room, usually where food is kept.

*grandfather clock* (89.25): an old-fashioned type of clock in a tall wooden case, which stands on the floor.

*oppressive* (89.26): uncomfortable.

*deliberate* (89.30): planned, intended.

*investigate* (89.31): find out about something.

*rumour* (89.31): information that may or may not be true.


# PARSON'S PLEASURE

## Focus

Mr Boggis pretends to be a clergyman. People would not suspect a clergyman of being dishonest and they would not think that a clergyman would ever be wealthy or be capable of or show any interest in making money. The story also makes use of a familiar situation in many literary fables and stories when less well-educated or unsophisticated country people misunderstand something important and the whole outcome of the story is affected.

There are contrasts in the way in which the characters in the story speak. Mr Boggis speaks standard British English while the workmen all speak in non-standard English dialects. The fact that Mr Boggis speaks in the standard dialect makes him sound educated and well informed. He would be less likely to be invited into people's homes if he spoke differently; his accent and speech style also make him sound much more like a typical, educated clergyman. For example: Mr Boggis says: 'I do apologize for troubling you, especially on a Sunday'; this contrasts with the regional, non-standard dialect of Claud who says: 'There ain't no chair in the world worth four hundred pound' (100.18, 100.34).

At the end of the story did Mr Boggis get what he deserved?

## Follow-up

List ten words connected with furniture which are used in the story. (For example: armchair, inlay, chest-of-drawers.)

Why does Mr Boggis disguise himself in the uniform of a clergyman?

Why does he not visit people who are very prosperous?

Why do people always let Mr Boggis into their homes?

Look at Mr Boggis's visiting card on p. 95. Why is it effective?

Why does Mr Boggis tell Rummins about a chair worth four hundred pounds?

Why is the 'Chippendale' chest-of-drawers a 'dealer's dream' to Mr Boggis?

Why does Mr Boggis say that he was only interested in the legs?

For what reasons does Mr Boggis say that the chest-of-drawers is a fake?

**Language Notes and Activities**

Why do Claud, Bert and Rummins saw the legs off the chest-of-drawers?

Should the story have given us Mr Boggis's reaction when he returned to collect the chest-of-drawers or is it better for the reader to be left to imagine it?

*Parson* (title): a Christian priest.

*primroses* (91.4): wild flowers.

*hawthorn* (91.5): a small tree or bush which has sharp thorns and white flowers.

*elevation* (91.13): raised up, not flat.

*it might be a Queen Anne* (91.23): the style suggesting that it might be a house built during the reign of Queen Anne, that is, between 1702 and 1714.

*Georgian house* (92.3): a house built in the Georgian period, that is, between 1714 and 1830.

*prosperous* (92.5): wealthy, having a lot of money.

*ruled it out* (92.6): rejected it as unsuitable.

*dilapidated* (92.15): old and in a bad condition.

*binoculars* (92.15): two small telescopes joined together side by side, which are looked through in order to see objects that are far away.

*sinister* (92.21): evil or harmful.

*a dealer in antique furniture* (92.22): a person who buys and sells old furniture which is valuable because of its beauty, or because it is rare.

*His premises* (92.23): the buildings where he did his business.

*obsequious* (92.30): too willing to obey or serve.

*mischievous* (92.31): acting as if wanting to have fun.

*arch* (92.31): playful.

*saucy* (92.31): rather cheeky, or rude, but in an amusing way.

*spinster* (92.32): a woman who is not married.

*clownish* (93.1): silly.

*inexhaustible* (93.17): never ending.

*fanbelt* (93.27): a rubber belt in a car engine that drives the fan which keeps the engine running.

*turned spindles* (94.2): narrow pieces of wood shaped on a wood-working machine called a lathe.

*inlay* (94.3): a design on the surface of the furniture made by putting pieces of other wood or metal into it, so that the resulting surface is smooth.

*Dear me* (94.14): an exclamation of surprise or confusion.

*bargained* (94.33): discussed prices until they reached an agreement.

*station-wagon* (94.36): a car with a long body, doors at the back and a space behind the back seats. It is now usually called an estate car.

*comb the countryside* (95.6): search the area thoroughly.

*counties* (95.9): regions which have their own local government. There are around thirty English counties. The names of the main counties around London are: Kent, Surrey, Essex and Middlesex.

*comparatively isolated* (95.15): more or less a long way from other buildings.

*home counties* (95.19): the area in the south-east of England around London.

*plumber* (95.27): a person who connects and repairs water and drainage pipes, baths, sinks and toilets.

*Reverend* (95.31): a title used to address a clergyman.

*inventory* (96.3): a detailed list.

*port* (96.13): a type of strong, sweet, red wine.

*lucrative* (96.19): making a lot of money.

*imbecility* (97.1): stupidity, silliness.

*dog-collar* (97.2): a stiff, white collar worn by clergymen in the Christian Church.

*rustic* (97.4): simple, related to the countryside or country people.

*whinny* (97.14): a noise made by a horse.

*Socialist Party* (97.23): a left-wing political organization which thinks that a country's resources and industries should be controlled by everybody, or by the State, and that wealth should be divided equally between everyone.

*Tory* (97.25): another word for a Conservative, that is, a member or supporter of the Conservative Party (see below).

*eulogy* (97.27): a speech of praise.

## Language Notes and Activities

*Conservative Party* (97.28): a right-wing political organization which supports free enterprise and the private ownership of industry.

*clincher* (97.29): something that is used as a way of finally settling an argument or discussion.

*Bill* (97.29): a formal proposal for a new law.

*bloodsports* (97.30): sports in which animals or birds are killed.

*guffaw* (98.4): a loud, noisy laugh.

*mahogany* (98.27): a type of dark, reddish-brown wood used for making furniture.

*veneered* (98.27): covered with a thin layer of good quality wood.

*lattices* (98.34): a frame of crossed strips with spaces in between.

*husk* (98.35): the outer covering.

*paterae* (98.35): specialist term describing a part of the chair.

*caning on the seat* (98.35): long, hollow stems of certain plants, woven together in order to form the seat of the chair.

*the legs were very gracefully turned* (98.36): the legs had been shaped (turned) on a woodworking machine called a lathe, in a very pleasing and attractive way.

*outward splay* (99.1): turned outwards.

*'give'* (99.6): the action of bending or stretching when weight or pressure is applied.

*infinitesimal* (99.7): the very smallest.

*degree of shrinkage* (99.7): the amount by which something becomes smaller, caused in this case by the wood drying out over many years.

*mortice and dovetail joints* (99.8): different ways in which two pieces of wood are joined together.

*leashes* (99.20): long, thin pieces of material, usually leather, which are fastened to dogs' collars in order to keep them under control.

*corrugated* (99.30): with a series of small folds or ridges.

*poke his nose into* (100.5): try to find out about.

*contemptuous* (100.13): showing a lack of respect.

*sneer* (100.14): a facial expression which shows dislike and a lack of respect.

*hobnailed boots* (101.4): heavy shoes with short nails put in underneath to make them wear out less quickly.

*larder* (101.12): a small room or cupboard where food is kept.

*alas* (101.20): an expression of sadness or regret.

*deal* (101.26): type of wood.

*goddamn* (102.10): a swear word which emphasizes the word which follows.

*fatuous leer* (102.17): a silly, foolish, but unpleasant look.

*wary* (102.28): cautious, aware of possible problems.

*a layman* (103.1): a person who is not qualified or experienced in a subject.

*coveted* (103.5): very much wanted or desired.

*guineas* (103.14): a guinea is a British unit of money (no longer used) worth twenty-one shillings.

*templates* (103.20): thin pieces of metal or wood used to help a person cut wood or metal accurately, or to make the same shape many times.

*luscious* (103.33): extremely attractive and, in this case, very profitable.

*rococo style* (104.7): a style of decoration using a curly design which was popular in the eighteenth century, that is, between 1700 and 1799.

*fluted legs* (104.8): legs which have grooves cut or shaped into them.

*serpentine* (104.11): a curved and winding shape, like the shape which a snake makes when it moves.

*intricate* (104.13): very detailed and complicated.

*festoons and scrolls and clusters* (104.13): types of design which are cut into the wood.

*reproduction* (104.33): a more modern copy of an old work of art.

*Victorian times* (104.33): during the reign of Queen Victoria, that is, between 1837 and 1901.

*craftsmanship* (105.4): the skill a person uses when he or she makes beautiful things, especially with his or her hands.

*Michaelmas* (105.15): the Christian festival of St Michael that takes place at the end of September.

*sermon* (105.17): a talk on a religious or moral subject.

*auction* (106.5): a sale where people offer higher and higher prices for something until it is sold.

## Language Notes and Activities

*Squire* (106.5): in former times the squire of an English village was the man who owned most of the land in it.

*rabbit-snares* (106.18): traps made from loops of wire which pull tight around the rabbits' legs.

*rummaging* (106.25): searching for something by moving things around in an untidy and careless way.

*brittle* (106.31): hard, but easily broken.

*copperplate* (106.32): a very neat and regular style of handwriting, where the letters are sloping and joined together by loops.

*carvd chasd* . . . (107.1): carved; chased. The 'e' has been missed out from both words because this was the usual way of writing in former times. 'Chased' means engraved with a design.

*ditto* (107.32): the same thing again.

*give the game away* (107.17): reveal something which is secret or private.

*varnish* (108.2): a liquid painted onto wood to give it a hard, shiny surface.

*processed* (108.8): treated with chemical substances.

*lime* (108.12): a chemical substance made by heating limestone.

*potash salts* (108.14): a chemical substance.

*walnut* (108.14): a type of wood.

*the grain* (108.19): the natural pattern of a piece of wood, the way that the lines run on the surface of the wood.

*patina* (108.23): a fine layer that forms on old wood, giving it a shiny appearance.

*linseed oil* (109.1): an oil put on wood to protect it.

*french polish* (109.1): a liquid painted on wood to give it a hard, shiny surface.

*pumice-stone* (109.3): a grey stone, which is very light, and is used to clean surfaces.

*beeswaxing* (109.3): polishing with a substance made from wax produced by bees.

*knavery* (109.6): dishonesty.

*fakers* (109.25): people who make things look valuable in order to cheat others.

*scoundrels* (110.1): people who behave in a bad way, especially by deceiving and cheating other people.

*sal ammoniac* (110.7): a chemical substance.

*lustre* (110.9): the gentle brightness of a smooth, shining surface.

*ironmonger's* (111.8): a shop which sells tools, nails, pans and other items.

*reckless* (112.5): showing a lack of care about danger or the results of one's actions.

*carcass* (112.16): the main body of the piece of furniture.

*haggle* (112.20): argue about the price.

*a jiffy* (112.33): a moment, a few seconds or minutes.

*sovereigns* (113.4): old coins made from gold.

*bastard* (113.20): a swear word, a rude and insulting way to refer to someone.

*to hell with it* (113.27): an expression meaning one does not care about something or want to have anything more to do with it.

*bovine* (114.5): like a cow.

*I reckon he's balmy* (114.21): I think that he's behaving in a strange and silly way ('balmy' would usually be written 'barmy').

*piddling* (115.3): small.

*Morris Eights or Austin Sevens* (115.3): types of car that are now no longer made.


## THE SOUND MACHINE

### Focus

Roald Dahl had a fascination with machines and machinery; similar scientific descriptions and ideas for machines occur in his stories for children, for example, *Charlie and the Chocolate Factory*, as well as in short stories such as 'William and Mary' and 'The Great Automatic Grammatizator'. The story also illustrates Dahl's interest in a world beyond our ordinary understanding.

Notice how Klausner frequently uses the language of science and discovery in his speech but also that at the same time he sounds like a Romantic. For example: 'an endless succession of notes . . . an infinity of notes . . . there is a note – if only our ears could hear it – so high that it vibrates a million times a second . . . and another a million times as high as that . . . and on and on, higher and higher, as far as numbers go, which is . . . infinity . . . eternity . . . beyond the stars' (118.27–32).

'There is a whole world of sound about us all the time that we cannot hear.' Do you agree with Klausner?

### Follow-up

What does Klausner keep in his garden shed and why does he at first not want to tell, Scott, the doctor, what it is?

What is Klausner's theory?

What does Klausner want to do with his sound machine?

What does he hear when Mrs Saunders cut the roses?

What does Mrs Saunders think of Klausner?

What does he hear when he starts to chop the tree trunk?

Why does he call Dr Scott? Did the doctor hear anything?

What happens to the sound machine?

What does Klausner do to the tree trunk?

Is Klausner mad? Is he a genius? Is he capable of inventing and seeing things which ordinary people are unable to do? Are most scientists mad? Why do we say people are mad?

Do you think Klausner will build another sound machine? Are there inventions which should be banned because they are so dangerous?

Does the story end too quickly? Do you want it to continue?

*interior* (116.6): the inside.
*workbench* (116.7): a type of table on which a person uses tools to make or repair things.

*coffin* (116.9): a box in which a dead body is placed.

*twiddle* (116.20): twist or turn quickly.

*mechanism* (116.21): the inside part of a machine that does a particular job.

*deftly* (116.24): skilfully, quickly.

*suppressed* (117.4): hidden, not outwardly expressed.

*How's that throat of yours been behaving?* (117.13): How does your throat feel, has it been working properly?

*innards* (117.25): things inside.

*distracted* (117.26): worried, or thinking about something else.

*Good heavens, man!* (117.32): a phrase expressing surprise or irritation.

*complexity* (118.2): having many connecting parts joined in a difficult and puzzling way.

*inquisitive* (118.4): wanting to find out about things.

*vibrations* (118.18): continuous rapid movements.

*animated* (118.33): lively, excited.

*steel spectacles* (119.2): glasses with steel rims.

*bewildered* (119.2): confused, puzzled.

*remote* (119.3): seeming far away.

*inaudible* (119.14): not able to be heard.

*subtle* (119.15): not directly noticeable or obvious.

*harmonies* (119.15): pleasant combinations of different notes of music.

*grinding discords* (119.15): unpleasant and harsh combinations of musical notes.

*too high-pitched for reception by the human ear* (120.3): the sounds are too high for the human ear to detect.

*average* (120.9): typical or normal.

*My goodness!* (120.18): an expression of surprise.

*I must fly* (120.19): I must hurry.

*Oh, my God* (120.26): a phrase used to emphasize the words which follow.

*lawn* (120.31): an area of grass in a garden, kept cut short.

*consumptive* (121.4): describing someone who looks weak, pale and thin, as if he or she was suffering from tuberculosis.

## Language Notes and Activities

*bespectacled* (121.4): wearing glasses.

*cocked* (121.16): at an angle.

*spasmodic* (121.19): happening at irregular intervals.

*tentacle* (121.24): a long thin flexible part that extends from the body of a creature like a snail or octopus.

*ultrasonic* (121.26): sounds which are so high in pitch that they cannot be heard by human beings.

*instinctively* (122.2): describing an action that is done without thinking logically about it.

*neighbour* (122.11): the person who lives next door.

*humour* (122.22): keep happy or please someone even though he or she is behaving in a strange or unreasonable way.

*daisy* (123.25): a small white flower.

*inanimate* (123.30): without life, not alive.

*toin or spurl or plinuckment* (124.2): words invented by the author in order to show how plants might express their feelings.

*pricks of light* (124.5): small points of light.

*coal cellar* (124.18): an underground room for storing coal.

*woodflesh* (124.35): the softer part of the trunk of the tree underneath the harder outer covering.

*gash* (125.1): a long, deep cut.

*consulted* (125.9): looked at.

*hysterical* (125.26): in a state of uncontrolled excitement, panic or fear.

*anchored* (126.2): fastened down.

*mower* (126.9): a machine for cutting grass.

*disturbed* (126.29): unhappy, upset.

*he could swear he. . .* (127.17): he was absolutely sure that he . . .

*Great heavens!* (127.33): an exclamation expressing great surprise or shock, used for emphasis.

*irritably* (128.15): in an angry or annoyed way.

*Oh hell!* (128.18): an expression of anger or annoyance, used for emphasis.

*For God's sake* (128.21): an exclamation used to emphasize what is being said.

*suffused* (128.28): spread all over with.

*threatening* (128.33): expressing an intention of doing harm or violence to someone or something.

*iodine* (129.2): a substance used on wounds to prevent infection.

## THE WISH

### Focus
Roald Dahl had extensive experience in writing for children and in exploring the minds of children. He wrote an autobiographical account of his own childhood in the book *Boy*. This story goes inside the mind of a young child and records the world through the imagination of that child. On one level the story may seem unreal but on another level it captures in a truthful and realistic manner the way in which children can sometimes want to make things happen.

The writer creates two voices in the story: the narrator and the boy. It is almost as if the narrator is listening to the boy's voice. For example: 'I'll be bitten and I'll die before tea time. And if I get across safely, without being burnt and without being bitten, I will be given a puppy for my birthday tomorrow. He got to his feet and climbed higher up the stairs to obtain a better view of this vast tapestry of colour and death' (132.2–6).

Why is the story called 'The Wish'?

### Follow-up
What does the child do to the scab on his knee?

What effect does the carpet first have on the child?

Why can he not walk on the red parts of the carpet?

What is he most afraid of as he walks across the carpet?

What does the snake 'with bright beady eyes' do?

What does the child see as he looks down at the black patterns of the carpet?

**Language Notes and Activities**

Does the child manage to cross the carpet?

What part does his mother play in the story?

The story is a symbolic story. The story is not simply about a child walking across a carpet. The actions of the child have to be interpreted. Do you like this type of story? Why?

Does the ending of the story make sense to you?

*scab* (131.1): a piece of hard skin which covers a wound or cut.
*gravely* (131.18): seriously.
*adders* (131.27): types of poisonous snake.
*cobras* (131.27): types of large, powerful, poisonous snake.
*fringe* (132.10): the front part of the hair cut short over the eyebrows.
*triumphantly* (132.14): successfully.
*sandalled* (132.21): wearing sandals (a type of open shoe).
*gingerly* (132.31): cautiously and carefully.
*windmill fashion* (132.35): moving arms like the sails of a windmill, a building that uses the wind to create power.
*beady* (133.26): hard and dark.
*jerked* (134.10): made a sudden sharp movement.
*doing the splits* (134.12): spreading his legs very widely apart.
*glister* (134.15): shining and glistening.
*frantically* (134.16): in a panic.
*instinctively* (134.19): unconsciously, by instinct.

# Further Activities and Study Questions

Suggest two other titles for the story 'The Umbrella Man'.

Do you like the story 'The Umbrella Man' being told through the eyes of a 12-year-old girl? Would it be improved if told from the mother's point of view? How would the story change if it were told from the point of view of the 'umbrella man?'

In 'The Umbrella Man' imagine that the mother goes to the police station to report the 'umbrella man'. The police ask her to appear on television in order to warn other people. Write out what you think she should say (70–100 words).

Imagine that you are Mr Botibol in the story 'Dip in the Pool' and that you write a daily diary just before you go to sleep each night. Write a diary entry for the day on which he buys his ticket in the auction.

Summarize in thirty words what happens at the end of the story 'Dip in the Pool'.

Consider the following alternative ending for the story 'Dip in the Pool'. The lady to whom Mr Botibol speaks and who sees him jump is not mad. She calls for help and the ship turns round and saves Mr Botibol. Write a new final paragraph for the story.

List ten words from the story 'The Butler' connected with wine or with the drinking of wine. For example, 'bouquet' (23.31). Using the following words of Tibbs from the story describe how you should taste wine: *sniff*; *air bubble*; *suck in air*; *roll vigorously around*; *swallow* (23.21–26).

'The butler' has applied for another post. Write a letter of recommendation for him. Make sure that you say both positive and negative things about him.

A friend of yours has been invited to one of Mr Cleaver's parties in 'The Butler' and has written to you to ask about Mr Cleaver. Write a reply (100 words) in which you write both (*a*) about his character and (*b*) about his appearance.

Would you employ a servant if you had enough money? What would be the most important servant for you? A butler? A cook? A driver? Think about the question with reference to 'The Butler'.

In 100 words write a summary of the dialogue between the policeman and the driver in 'The Hitchhiker'. Use your own words.

Write a description of (*a*) the car; (*b*) the hitchhiker; (*c*) the policeman (50 words each).

Write a character description of the driver from the point of view of the hitchhiker.

List ten words from the story 'Mr Botibol' which are connected with music. For example: *concerto, choir*.

Look at these words from the story 'Mr Botibol' which describe Mr Botibol's appearance and character and his role as a conductor of an orchestra: *ovation; dais; baton; meek; self-effacing; melancholy; enraptured; tempo; grave; retiring*. Put them under the correct heading of either 'Appearance/character' or 'Conductor'.

Mr Botibol writes a short article for a music magazine about the experience of conducting. What will he say? Write 100 words.

Write a letter from Miss Darlington to a friend in which she describes her first meeting with Mr Botibol (100–150 words).

List ten words from the story 'My Lady Love, My Dove' which are connected with cards and playing cards.

Imagine that Sally Snape keeps a diary. Write her entry for their first day at Arthur and Pamela's house (150 words).

Write a paragraph describing how Arthur feels about his wife, Pamela (100 words).

Why does the story have the title 'My Lady Love, My Dove'? Suggest two other titles for the story.

Do you think the reader is meant to feel sorry for Sally Snape?

List ten words from the story 'The Way up to Heaven' which describe Mrs Foster as being either nervous or afraid. For example: *flutter, fidget*.

Write a short letter from Mrs Foster to her daughter in Paris. Describe what happened when she returned home and describe Mrs Foster's plans for the future (100 words).

Write a short letter from Mr Foster to his daughter. Describe his reactions to his wife's trips to the airport.

Imagine that Mr Boggis in 'Parson's Pleasure' writes a newspaper advertisement for his services. What will he say? (50 words).

Write out a dialogue between Boggis and Rummins when he returns to find that the legs have been sawn off.

Why are people so easily fooled by Mr Boggis?

List ten words from the story 'The Sound Machine' which are connected with sound. For example: *vibration, note*.

The list of words below are taken from the story 'The Sound Machine', describing an absence of sound or physical pain: *gash*; *screaming*; *shriek*; *cut*; *toneless*; *wound*; *stony*; *inaudible*. Put them under the correct heading of either 'Absence of sound' or 'Physical pain'.

Write a letter from Mrs Saunders to a friend in which she describes her encounter with Klausner from 'The Sound Machine' (70–100 words).

What will happen the next day after the story 'The Sound Machine' finishes? Write 70–100 words.

Imagine that Dr Scott in 'The Sound Machine' phones a fellow doctor for advice about Klausner. Write a dialogue of about 15 sentences.

Suggest a different title for the story which refers to Klausner rather than to the sound machine.

How well does Dahl describe sounds in 'The Sound Machine'? Give examples.

Do you ever imagine that if you overcome some fearful task you will get a reward? Were the snakes in the story 'The Wish' real snakes? Did you play similar games to this in your childhood? Why? Why not?

Have you ever wished for something and then played an imaginary game to see whether you can have it or not?

Imagine the mother in 'The Wish' is watching the boy. What is her reaction? Write about 70 words describing what she sees and how she feels about it.

Write three sentences, especially for a young child who is reading this kind of story for the first time. What would you say to help an understanding of the story?

---

Is the 'umbrella man' in the story 'The Umbrella Man' a criminal? Should he go to prison for his crimes? Compare the criminality of the 'umbrella man' with the crimes committed by other characters in these stories.

Would the story 'My Lady Love, My Dove' be improved if it were narrated by Pamela? Write an account of the importance of point of view in two other stories in this collection.

Do you like stories, like 'The Hitchhiker', which keep the reader constantly guessing? Give reasons for or against.

Do you sympathize or not with Mrs Foster in the story 'The Way up to Heaven'? In the collection as a whole does Dahl create mainly sympathetic or unsympathetic characters?

With reference to at least three stories discuss the theme of cruelty in these stories.

Do you agree that for the most part adults in these stories behave like children?

## Character Notes
There is insufficient character development in short stories of this type to merit a separate section devoted to characters in the stories but please refer to the section 'Further activities and study questions' where there is some related guidance.

# Text Summaries

## The Umbrella Man

After visiting the dentist in London, a 12-year-old girl and her mother prepare to return home. It is raining hard and there are no taxis available. An old man with an umbrella approaches them and tells them that he has forgotten his wallet. He offers to let the woman have his silk umbrella, which is worth £20, in exchange for £1, so that he can get a taxi home. The woman is suspicious but the man seems well dressed and well spoken, so after some discussion, the woman agrees. The old man hurries away. The woman and girl think that he might be up to something and decide to follow him. He enters a public house, hangs up his hat and coat, and orders a treble whisky. The woman and girl watch through a large window. As the old man leaves, he collects his hat, coat and someone else's umbrella. The woman and girl then realize that the old man has tricked them when they see him approach another person who is getting wet and again offer to exchange the newly stolen umbrella for £1.

## Dip in the Pool

The story takes place on a large passenger ship. After a spell of rough weather, the sea has calmed. During dinner, the weather becomes violent again. Mr Botibol, one of the passengers, wonders whether the ship's captain had made his estimate of how far the ship will travel in a day before the weather became rough again. When questioned, the purser, one of the crew, tells Botibol that he thinks that the captain made his estimate during the period of calm weather. The passengers hold an auction each night and bid for numbers corresponding to the number of miles travelled. The number closest to the actual amount travelled wins all the money in the pool, so the captain's estimate is important in deciding which number to bid for. Mr Botibol goes up on deck, but the weather is so bad that he returns inside and questions another crew member who tells him that the ship has definitely slowed down.

Mr Botibol dreams of buying a car if he wins the auction pool. Then the captain reveals his estimate and the auction begins. Ten numbers either side of the estimate make up the range, but people can also bid for high field and low field numbers. Bidding takes place and numbers close to the estimate are sold at around £110 each. A low field number comes up. This represents every number below the smallest number in the range. After some tense bidding, Mr Botibol secures it for around £200, which is all the money that he has in his bank account. He goes to bed in a contented mood when he finds out that the money in the pool is £5,400.

The next morning, the weather is very calm. Mr Botibol begins to panic as he has spent all his money on a low number in the auction. Now, because of the change in the weather, he thinks that the ship will increase its speed and a high number will surely win. He decides to jump overboard, so that the ship will have to turn back to rescue him. As he prepares to jump, he notices an elderly woman further along the deck. He thinks that she will be able to summon help after his fall. However, he is nervous, and decides to approach her to make sure that she has seen him. Worrying that she may be the owner of a high number and thus reluctant to raise the alarm, he questions her about the auction. She says that she knows nothing about it, as she always goes to bed early. Satisfied, Mr Botibol leaves her and plunges into the sea. The woman sees him fall and hears his shouts for help, but she seems unable to know what to do. She sees Mr Botibol's head bobbing in the water, and watches him as the ship goes further and further away.

After some time, another woman comes up on deck looking for the elderly lady, who tells her about Mr Botibol's fall. The second woman does not believe her, despite her protestations. She speaks sharply, reprimanding her for wandering and, finally, leads her away.

## The Butler

After George Cleaver has made a lot of money, he and his wife move into an elegant London house. They employ a French chef, Monsieur Estragon, and an English butler, Tibbs. The Cleavers want to move up in society, so they give many lavish dinner parties, but these are not totally successful. Tibbs claims that this is because the cheap wine which is served does not complement the superb food. He then advises Mr Cleaver on the best, most expensive wines and is instructed to search for and buy them. Mr Cleaver himself then becomes interested in wine. He reads all about it and learns from his butler. Eventually, he becomes something of an expert, but bores everyone with his supposed knowledge.

When his guests still seem unappreciative, Cleaver again asks Tibbs's advice and is told that the guests cannot taste the wine as Mr Cleaver insists on too much vinegar in the salad dressing. Cleaver thinks this is nonsense and mocks his butler about it later, in front of some dinner guests. He claims that he can taste the wine that he is drinking and that he recognizes it to be a very expensive one. Tibbs replies that it is cheap red wine, and tells him that he has only ever served him this cheap wine because Mr Cleaver has ruined his palate and might as well drink dishwater. In front of the astounded guests, the butler goes on to inform Cleaver that he and the chef have appreciated and enjoyed drinking all the expensive wines which had been bought. Tibbs then leaves, joining the chef, who is already packing their luggage into their small car.

## The Hitchhiker

The narrator is driving up to London in his new sports car, of which he is very proud. He sees a hitchhiker and stops to give him a lift. The hitchhiker tells the driver that he is going to Epsom race-course, because a big horse race, the Derby, is taking place there. The driver asks the hitchhiker if he works at the race-course, or bets on horses. The man replies that he does neither but is in a highly skilled trade. They talk for a while about the driver's occupation, which is writing, and about the car. The hitchhiker is sceptical of the claims made about how fast the car can travel. So the driver demonstrates by going faster and faster. Eventually, they are stopped by a police motorcyclist and charged with speeding. The policeman writes the driver a speeding ticket and asks the hitchhiker for his identity as he may be needed as a witness. The hitchhiker gives him a name and address and shows him a driving licence.

Before he departs the policeman tells the driver that he is in serious trouble and may end up in prison. The driver is worried, but is consoled by the hitchhiker who says that it is likely he will only be fined. Relieved, the driver then asks why the hitchhiker told the policeman that he was unemployed. He replies that it is because his trade is a rather peculiar one and he does not like talking about it. He goes on to boast about his skilful fingers. The driver is intrigued. The hitchhiker then demonstrates his skill by producing the driver's belt, shoelace, watch and various other personal items which he had removed during the course of the journey without the driver noticing. He says that he prefers not to be called a pickpocket, but sees himself as a professional 'fingersmith' and, what is more, he has never been caught. At this point, the driver reminds him that the policeman has all their details in his notebooks and is bound to check up on them. The hitchhiker then produces the notebooks which he has taken from the policeman and suggests that they stop the car and burn them.

### Mr Botibol

Mr Botibol meets Mr Clements, a solicitor, in a hotel. Clements is negotiating the purchase of Mr Botibol's company. They discuss their business over drinks. After the negotiations are over, Mr Botibol tells Clements that he has never had a single success in the whole of his life. He is insistent on this point and irritates Clements because of his apparent self-pity.

They part and Botibol returns home. As he feels slightly drunk, he decides to listen to a symphony on the radio. As he listens, he becomes so involved with the music that he imagines that he is the conductor and pretends to conduct the orchestra. Later that same evening, after drinking wine with his dinner, he again listens to the radio and pretends to be a famous conductor. He finds this very exhilarating and decides to convert one of his rooms into a sort of concert-hall. He also buys a record player so that he is not dependent on finding suitable music on the radio. The room is converted and the equipment is installed. Even the sound effects of applause are bought, in order to re-create the atmosphere of a live concert.

After several performances, Mr Botibol becomes totally immersed in his make-believe world and feels confident and successful. As he now likes to pretend that he is both a famous conductor and a famous composer, he decides to buy a concert piano. He orders a piano that makes no sound when it is played, because a record will supply the necessary music. Mr Botibol wants to pretend that he is Chopin. He then visits a record shop and begins talking to a rather plain-looking woman, Miss Darlington, who is also choosing records of Chopin's music. He invites her to his home.

Miss Darlington arrives at Mr Botibol's house. He is worried about her reaction to his concert hall but decides to show it to her. He explains everything and tells her about the pleasure he receives from pretending that he is a composer, because he feels that only a composer can get the maximum enjoyment from his music. Miss Darlington is rather puzzled by his enthusiasm. She thinks that her imagination cannot be as strong as that of Mr Botibol. Mr Botibol suggests that they perform together; she can pretend to play the piano, while he pretends to conduct. She feels that this is rather stupid, but nevertheless agrees to return later, dressed for the occasion. Later that evening, the pretend concert takes place and Miss Darlington is surprised to find that afterwards she is as elated as Mr Botibol. Finally, Mr Botibol is rather upset when Miss Darlington reveals that she is actually a piano teacher. However, she agrees to return for further performances, saying that she has always wanted to be a famous pianist.

## My Lady Love, My Dove

Arthur and his wife, Pamela, are discussing some guests they are expecting for the weekend. The guests are a couple called Henry and Sally Snape. Pamela does not like them very much because she thinks that they are social climbers. She has invited them because they are expert card players. Arthur, who is rather intimidated by his wife, thinks that they are a nice young couple, but his wife contradicts him.

Pamela decides to have some fun at the Snapes' expense. She plans to put a microphone in their bedroom so that she can listen to their private conversation. Arthur thinks this is a very nasty trick. However, after a short argument, he agrees to his wife's plan. He is in the process of installing the microphone when the guests arrive and hurriedly completes the task. After calming himself, he joins the guests and gains the impression that they are very charming. He thinks that his wife may have been hasty in her judgement of them. After dinner, they all play cards for money. Henry and Sally play very well and only make one mistake which seems to upset Sally very much.

Eventually, it is time for bed. Arthur and Pamela turn the speakers on in their bedroom so that they can listen to what the couple are saying. They hear Henry shouting at Sally, blaming her for the mistake which cost them money. He tells her that they she must practise more. As Arthur and Pamela continue to listen, they realize that Henry and Sally have devised a secret bidding code which enables them to cheat at cards. Instead of being horrified, Pamela thinks that this is a good idea and sends her husband off to find a pack of cards so that they, too, can learn how to do it.

## The Way up to Heaven

Mr and Mrs Foster live in a large, gloomy house in New York and have few visitors. All her life Mrs Foster, who is not a particularly nervous person, has had a great dread of being late. This has grown into almost an obsession and irritates Mr Foster. Yet he seems to add to her suffering by always keeping her waiting. It is almost as if he enjoys doing this.

One January morning, Mr and Mrs Foster are preparing to leave for the airport. As usual, Mrs Foster is panicking about being late and Mr Foster is keeping her waiting. She is going to France to visit her daughter and grandchildren. Mr Foster is accompanying her to the airport and then moving into his club while she is away, as the house is being shut up. The weather is very foggy and when they arrive at the airport, the flight has been postponed. Mrs Foster decides to wait and her husband returns to the city. After waiting all day, Mrs Foster is told that the flight will not now leave until eleven the following morning. She telephones home. Her husband has not yet left for his club and he insists that she return to the house for the night, saying that he will stay with her and she can drop him at his club on her way to the airport the following morning.

Next morning, Mrs Foster is ready to leave at eight-thirty. Once again, Mr Foster keeps her waiting and she begins to worry. Finally, they get into the car, but Mr Foster cannot find a present that he has for his daughter. He is sure that he brought it with him but cannot find it, so he returns to the house to search for it. Time passes and Mrs Foster is sure that she will miss the plane. Then she notices the present tucked down the side of the car seat. She rushes to the house and is about to enter, but stops and listens closely at the door. Then, all at once she returns to the car and tells the driver to hurry to the airport as she cannot wait any longer and Mr Foster must get a taxi to his club. She manages to catch the plane with a few minutes to spare.

After spending six weeks with her daughter and grandchildren, Mrs Foster returns home. She seems much calmer than before. As she enters the dank, cold house, she sees a large pile of mail behind the door and notices that there is a strange smell. Mrs Foster walks swiftly about the hall and appears to be investigating or confirming something. She then goes to her husband's study, telephones and asks for someone to come as soon as possible to repair the elevator which seems to be stuck between two floors. She sits and waits patiently for the arrival of the repair man.

## Parson's Pleasure

Mr Boggis is a very knowledgeable but not very honest antique dealer. He disguises himself as a clergyman, because he thinks this will make him seem trustworthy, and claims to be the president of the Society for the Preservation of Rare Furniture. In his disguise, he travels around the countryside and buys antiques for far less than they are worth. The idea for this came to him when his car broke down in the country and he had to ask for help at a farmhouse, where he noticed some valuable chairs. He was able to buy them at a twentieth of their value.

One Sunday, Mr Boggis is, as usual, travelling around. He visits two houses. At the first, he finds nothing of value. At the second, he sees a valuable chair and table through the window. As there is no one in, he plans to return later.

After parking his rather large estate car some distance away so as not to arouse suspicion, he calls at a farmhouse. Here, he encounters three men: Mr Rummins, the owner of the farm, Bert, his son, and a neighbour named Claud. The men are dubious of Boggis who pretends that he is not really interested in buying as he has very little money, but only wants to write about any treasures which he might find. After some persuasion, Rummins lets him look inside the house. Boggis sees an extremely rare and valuable piece of furniture, one of only four in existence. It is a type of chest-of-drawers called a Chippendale Commode. Boggis is very excited, but in order not to arouse the men's suspicions, he pretends to be scornful about this piece of furniture. Eventually he claims that although it is of very little value, the legs from the chest-of-drawers might be useful to him because he has a coffee table whose legs are damaged. Casually, he offers to buy the piece of furniture. Mr Rummins is not sure, because he thinks that it might be older and more valuable than Mr Boggis is suggesting. To demonstrate this, he produces a bill which has been found in the chest-of-drawers. This proves that it is as genuine and as valuable as Boggis thought. Boggis is even more excited and takes great pains to persuade Rummins that it is a fake and a reproduction. He does this by showing them how furniture is made to look older and more valuable than it really is. After some bargaining, Rummins agrees to sell for £20.

Boggis leaves to fetch his car, rejoicing in his good fortune. While he is away, the three men think that it is unlikely that the chest-of-drawers will fit in Boggis's car, as they assume that a clergyman will only have a small vehicle. They decide to cut the legs off the chest-of-drawers as they think that this will save Boggis the job of doing it himself. Afterwards, they still think the furniture looks too large to fit into a car, so they chop it up into small pieces. This takes some effort and causes one of them to remark that, despite what Mr Boggis has said, the furniture seems to have been made by a very good carpenter. At this point, with the priceless piece of furniture in small pieces, they see Mr Boggis returning.

## The Sound Machine

Klausner is working on a strange machine in his garden shed. He is visited by Scott, a doctor, who enquires whether Klausner's throat is better. The doctor becomes intrigued by the device and examines it. Klausner tells him that it has something to do with sound. Scott questions him further. Klausner explains that a human can only hear a very small range of sounds, but beyond this is an infinity of sounds. He claims that his machine is able to pick up vibrations that are too high-pitched for normal human hearing, and tells him that he intends to test it that evening. The doctor seems sceptical and leaves.

Klausner takes his machine into the garden. He puts on headphones, switches on and turns the dial higher and higher. Suddenly, he hears a shriek. He thinks that it must be the woman who is cutting flowers in the garden next door, but she seems unperturbed. When it happens once more, he realizes that the scream occurs at the very moment the flower stem is cut. He tries to explain this to the woman, who is alarmed by his behaviour and goes inside. Klausner continues listening. He picks a daisy and hears a cry as the flower is plucked.

Next morning, Klausner tries another experiment. He sets up the machine in the park. He then takes an axe and chops at a tree trunk. This time he hears a terrible, long-drawn-out sob, which distresses him greatly. He rushes home, telephones the doctor and asks him to come over quickly because there has been an accident. While waiting, Klausner imagines the kinds of sounds which all the other plants might make. When the doctor arrives, Klausner leads him to the park, makes him put on the headphones, then takes the axe and swings at the tree. A loud cracking sound is heard and a great branch falls, missing Klausner, but smashing the machine. When questioned, the doctor claims only to have heard the cracking sound and no other noise. Klausner becomes very distressed and wants the doctor to sew up the cut in the tree. When he is told that this is impossible, he demands that the cut be painted with iodine. The doctor thinks this is ridiculous, but agrees as Klausner, with the axe in his hand, seems menacing. After the iodine has been applied, Klausner insists that the process is repeated next day. Only when this request is agreed to does he drop the axe. With a wild, excited smile on his face Klausner is gently, but quickly, led away by the doctor.

## The Wish

A child picks the scab off an old cut, flicks it away and it lands on the edge of an enormous red, black and yellow carpet which the child has never taken much notice of before. He imagines that the red parts of the carpet are red-hot lumps of coal and that the black parts are poisonous snakes. He tells himself that if he can cross the carpet without touching either the red or the black parts, he will be given a puppy as a birthday present.

The boy then attempts, very carefully, to cross the carpet by only treading on the yellow parts. Halfway across, he panics as there seems to be only great expanses of black before him. Standing on the only available patch of yellow, his foot seems very close to the black. A snake stirs and watches his foot. Another snake joins the first. The child is terrified and cannot move for some time. To reach the next yellow patch, he must cross a broad band of black. He contemplates jumping, but decides to stride over. Astride the black expanse, he finds that he is stuck. He looks down and appears to see a deep, swirling, writhing river of black beneath him. He loses his balance and puts a hand out to save himself. The hand plunges right into the middle of the glistening black mass and he cries out. Outside, far away from the house, the mother is looking for her son.

# Suggestions for Further Reading

The following critical biography is strongly recommended. It is clearly written, contains a wealth of biographical information and offers a number of perceptive insights into Dahl's writing for adults and for children.

Treglown, Jeremy, *Roald Dahl* (London, 1994).

# Audio Extracts

Approx. running time = 60 mins.